# CODA FOR A STAR

Shadows *of the* 'Summer of Love'

## Martin Horrocks

Ituri

**www.ituri.co.uk**

**Coda for a Star** is published by
**Ituri Publications**
Edge House
Kings Nympton EX37 9ST

**www.ituri.co.uk**

**ISBN 9780992965839**

© Martin Horrocks, 2016
The moral rights of the author have been asserted
A CIP record for this book is available from the British Library

**The characters and events depicted in this novel are fictitious. No resemblance is intended to actual persons or to real events other than those that provide the period context.**

Cover design by Book Production Services, London
**www.bookproductionservices.co.uk**

Front cover picture, festival time © iStockphoto.com/gilaxia
Front cover picture, cine film reel © iStockphoto.com/MarsBars
Back cover picture © iStockphoto.com/Druvo

Set in 10pt on 12pt Century Schoolbook with titles in Helvetica by Book Production Services

Printed and bound in the UK by 4edge Ltd
www.4edge.co.uk

**All rights reserved. This publication or any section of it may not be reproduced, stored in a retrieval system, or transmitted in any form or by any means (electronic, mechanical, photocopying, recording or otherwise) without the prior written permission of the publisher**

# Contents

Part One: Howard / 1
Part Two: Meg / 49
Part Three: Justice / 105

# PART ONE: HOWARD
# ONE

HOWARD settled himself in the easy chair in his spacious office. The chair along with his large desk was considerately placed at the side of the window, so visitors didn't have to face him half-blinded with the light behind him. He wouldn't subject them to that old trick.

'Fire away,' he told the young man, who was the brightest of the *Messenger*'s graduate recruits. He had come for an 'in-house' interview – that is, to interview Sir Howard Jenkins, chairman of Messenger Publications, for an article to mark his fifty years with the newspaper.

'Sir Howard, you've been with the *Messenger* for fifty years,' the lad began, setting up the question in the way beloved of interviewers, by telling the subject what he already knows. 'Is that a record in provincial journalism, do you know?'

Howard didn't care for the 'provincial journalism', but decided to ignore it.

'A record for the *Messenger* at any rate. And just "Howard" will do,' he said. 'We're all in the same team here.' He wondered about that 'in'. Did it make him sound dated, the old fossil image he wanted to avoid at seventy? Youngsters these days seemed to say 'on the team'. The American influence, he supposed.

'Very well, Howard,' the lad responded, using the name more comfortably than the chairman had expected and privately hoped for. 'Most people head for London at the first chance they get, but you stayed. I wondered why.'

'I was in London for awhile. I was with the *Sentinel*. But I came back. I prefer it here.' He hoped the boy hadn't picked up on the calamitous circumstances surrounding the Honourable Meg Denby, film star, and how he had returned to the *Messenger* beaten and broken. The reporter registered no special interest in his reasons.

'So strictly speaking it's not fifty years with the *Messenger*,' he said.

'I wasn't in London very long and we don't need to be too literal!' Howard replied with what he hoped was a conspiratorial smile from one journalist to another.

The reporter could hardly gainsay his chairman even if he had wanted to. He went on: 'So what would you say was your best achievement at the *Messenger*?'

Howard had of course expected this favourite journalistic question. Preparing for this interview the previous evening, he struggled to find anything that would look neither boring nor boastful in print. There were few incidents of the remotest outside interest to be found in the long years of editing copy and, latterly, attending managerial meeting after meeting. As a younger man he hadn't been a war correspondent, able to reel off anecdotes by the yard, or even a road-going reporter much beyond Batley and Huddersfield. He couldn't properly say his best moment was being elevated to the chairman's office after he retired as editor, or being awarded his knighthood 'for services to regional journalism'. Services to sticking around, as irreverent voices in the newsroom put it.

'I suppose my best moment was being close enough to my readers as editor to hear at first hand about their concerns and what they thought about the paper,' he said. In fact, the city was big enough that he could usually walk down the street unrecognised while those he met at events had mostly taken the opportunity to complain rather than praise. The reporter showed no interest in any of this.

'When the Queen came to open our new offices, that was pretty exciting,' Howard offered. A sudden thought came to his rescue. 'Even though the building was new, we refurbished the ladies' toilet on the first floor for her. Added a touch of luxury, you know.'

The reporter took up his pen, which had been unemployed for some time, and began to scribble. 'Did she use it?' he asked.

'Oh yes,' said Howard.

'Did she make any comment afterwards?'

'No.'

The reporter glanced at the many framed photographs on the chairman's wall, several of the royal visit among them. 'Apart from the Queen, who was the most famous visitor you welcomed here as editor?' he asked.

Howard tried to think of someone who would interest the readership. 'We had Sir Tim Berners-Lee,' he replied. The reporter looked puzzled. 'The inventor of the worldwide web,' Howard explained. The reporter would have preferred Joan Collins.

'Can I take another tack now?' he said. 'You started here in the Swinging Sixties. What can you tell me about them?'

Here was a subject about which Howard could have talked for hours. He tried to think what might interest the reporter.

'It was a very optimistic time, of course' he began, 'but

it was still also an old-fashioned time. Here on the newspaper there were no computers, for example. The noise of all the typewriters in the newsroom was amazing. Compositors had to re-type your copy all over again to produce lines of metal, which were then turned into printing plates. It was time-consuming and a nightly struggle.'

To the reporter it must have seemed a bizarre process. 'So you don't regret those days?'

'I do not, but what I miss about the Sixties are the fashions and the beautiful tunes. No one seems to produce melodies now. And the miniskirt was new then. That was when we discovered girls' legs.'

He wondered whether to say more about the sex thing. Well, he'd show the youngster that he was still alive to the idea of sex.

'The biggest single thing, I suppose, was the Pill. That started in the Sixties. Before that it was entirely normal to avoid sex before marriage. Probably most girls were virgins until they got married. Even those with steady boyfriends mostly didn't go all the way.'

He could see the young man was deeply shocked at the idea. 'It's hard to imagine a world like that,' he said.

'People were afraid of pregnancy, you see. Being a single mother was a terrible stigma. Girls were disowned by their families or forced to put the baby up for adoption. Landlords wouldn't rent accommodation to single mothers – that sort of thing.

'The Pill changed all that. Suddenly there was no reason not to – you know ... Living together became commonplace.'

Don't mention Meg Denby, Howard told himself. That would take them into an area where he didn't want to go. 'For me the Swinging Sixties are summed up by the gorgeous Julie Christie in a miniskirt and her film *Darling*. It's all there.'

'Who's Julie Christie?' the reporter asked.

They talked about Howard's knighthood and 'the secret of your distinguished career'. It didn't seem very distinguished to Howard but others must have thought so, hence the knighthood. Unless it was true what they said about 'services to sticking around'.

'I see the knighthood, which was wholly unexpected by the way, as recognition for the whole team here, not just me,' he answered sententiously. 'And also, I suppose, it was for my work with the Newspaper Society representing the interests of the regional press nationwide.'

'Well yes, what about the future of the regional press? The internet, blogs, social media and all that. Howard, do you tweet yourself?'

The question sounded faintly obscene to Howard. 'I don't tweet ... too long in the tooth for that!' he answered with a smile intended to convey that he absolutely wasn't. 'But I completely accept the importance of digital media. Newspapers are no longer only about print or mainly about print.' More's the pity, he wanted to add, but didn't.

'We ought to talk about what you see as the challenges facing the regional press at this time,' said the reporter with obvious reluctance. Howard slipped easily into presentation mode. His interlocutor dutifully made notes while the audio recorder did its work in the background. They then transited to the subject of Howard's personal life, this being a biographical piece.

'My wife Cynthia and I are heading for another fiftieth – our fiftieth wedding anniversary,' Howard said.

'Are you going to do something madcap for that?'

What a charming old-fashioned word, 'madcap', Howard thought. Amazing how these old words bounce from generation to generation, even unto the Twitter and Facebook era. 'I don't think so ... Lady Jenkins doesn't go in for "madcap". Nor do I,' he added hastily. How Cynthia had joked about her new appellation! She'd become used to it, however.

'But no children?'

'Sadly, no children.'

The lad, who would have no idea of the pain of a childless married couple, didn't pursue this. 'What about hobbies?'

Howard would like to have offered bungee jumping or abseiling; even caving if his arthritic hips and knees hadn't precluded it. 'My garden is a very hard taskmaster,' he said.

'Do you show at your village fete?'

'I'm afraid not.'

'Do you take part in the open gardens scheme?'

'I wouldn't dare.'

They both seemed to have run out of puff at this point. 'Well,' said the reporter, 'I think I've got what I need – together with background material, of course. Is there anything you'd like to add?'

Howard was ready for this classic question. He'd asked it often enough in his time as a reporter. Rarely had anyone come up with anything worthwhile. At least he could offer the reporter a cliché to end on.

'I'm confident that the *Messenger* has a bright future in this digital age, and I'm excited still to be part of it. In fact, I'm as excited to be working at the *Messenger* now as I was when I started here fifty years ago.'

It wasn't actually true, but who cared? Triteness was expected in anniversary articles. The last shall be first. He would bet money that the comment would become the intro. He was pleased with this final exchange but, as he drove back to his house on the edge of the city, he became increasingly dissatisfied with the rest of the interview. He had managed to make his career sound even more boring than it had been in reality, he told himself as he turned the car into the drive. How on earth was the reporter to get a thousand words out of that?

The house once belonged to Mr and Mrs Snelgrove – a fine Edwardian property of local stone, with two principal storeys and an attic floor lit by dormer windows. The Snelgroves had been among the glitziest members of local society in Howard's young days. It was at their house where he had his first proper conversation with Meg Denby, on a magical evening kissed by moonlight. Howard had always liked that house. He didn't know whether he liked it for itself or because of Meg, but when the chance to buy it came up twenty years previously he did so. It was ridiculous really, he and Cynthia alone in a property with five bedrooms and three acres of grounds (including a rose garden and lawns on two levels).

It would have been different, or slightly different, if Cynthia had liked to entertain or had weekend guests. But she didn't. Every summer they held a garden party attended by sundry county VIPs from the lord lieutenant downwards. At Christmas they invited the neighbours in for drinks, joined by a selected few from the *Messenger*. And that was about it.

Cynthia was waiting for him with a reviving glass of

merlot as usual. Howard got his question in first.

'How was your day at the University of the Third Age, Cyn?'

'Only all right,' his wife replied. 'There's a limit to my interest in Spanish irregular verbs. And yours, Howie?'

He'd never told Cynthia that he wasn't especially comfortable with 'Howie'. His was one of those names where no obvious diminutive offered itself. Perhaps that had been his parents' plan. If so, they had succeeded, apart from Cynthia.

'My day? About the same as yours. I did this interview for the article about my fifty years with the paper. I'm afraid I didn't give the reporter much. I must have sounded like a boring old stick.'

'You are a boring old stick,' she said, ruffling what remained of his hair.

'Seriously, Cyn, it doesn't seem like much when I look back at it all.'

'Don't get all introspective on me, dearest. You started as a trainee reporter; now you're chairman of the company. You're a knight of the realm. We have this magnificent house.'

'Is that all that matters?'

'Of course not,' Cynthia said, 'but they are all ways from which we know how others judge us.'

'It's still not enough. What of the journalists on the *Messenger*? Do you think they're impressed with all that?'

His wife moved to his side of the table and pushed him on to a chair. 'Look me in the eyes and listen to me,' she said. 'You should be beyond concerns of that sort. You know you can write good articles. You've done it often enough.'

But Howard wasn't even sure that was true. He wasn't to be shaken out of his bad day at the office. 'Do you know, I couldn't think of a single exciting story I covered as a reporter. I suppose there must have been some, but I never had the big story to dine out on, as they say. Who wants to know about management meetings and endless trips to London for the Newspaper Society? The best I could offer was how we re-did the ladies' lavatory for the Queen's visit – and I couldn't even say she got locked in it!'

Cynthia smiled. 'There you are then. The reporter will get something out of that. I prescribe another glass of merlot to cheer you up, Howard Jenkins.'

Good old Cynthia. Ever-practical Cynthia. She was always able to look on the bright side. He supposed it came from her active lifestyle. Unlike Howard, she didn't spend hours each day staring at a computer screen or listening to people taking five words where one would do at business meetings. She had always been sporty, since the days when they were teenagers in Bristol. She still played tennis three days a week. She was the leader of a ladies' baking circle. She did tapestry and cross-stitch. Her nearest approach to an intellectual pursuit was the University of the Third Age, where she had decided to learn Spanish.

'It will open the door to South America for us,' she had enthused.

Howard had bitten his lip. 'Except Brazil' was all he replied.

After pouring the merlot, Cynthia continued, 'And my second prescription is to go for a ride on that lovely sit-on mower of yours. You know how you enjoy it.'

It was true. Cutting the grass invariably restored his

good humour. He had always liked the idea of a sit-on mower, and eventually he found himself with lawns big enough for one. Sometimes he felt happier on the mower than in the big BMW sitting in the drive. That was absurd, Howard admonished himself. He must keep a sense of proportion. He'd be falling in love with a bicycle next!

An hour on the mower took care of the lower lawn. Rob, the contract gardener hired by the hour, could deal with the edges and borders. It meant they were later than usual for supper, for which Cynthia had cooked a casserole.

'Very tasty, very sweet,' said Howard appreciatively as he cleared his plate.

'You always say that,' his wife replied.

'Well, it always is.'

'I mean the same expression – "very tasty, very sweet".'

'It's just something my father always said. I must have picked it up from him.'

'As a matter of fact, "sweet" is what it wasn't,' Cynthia pursued. 'It had a good amount of chilli to perk it up.'

Howard knew the exchange wasn't yet terminated. It needed to be finished. 'I didn't mean it literally,' he said, after which they both resorted to silence.

The ritual of the 10pm TV news soon followed. It presented the usual diet of gloom and doom at home and abroad concluding with a light, human interest item. But short of a revolution, an air crash of unbearable horror or the abolition of income tax, little shook Cynthia out of her news ennui. 'Nothing much of interest tonight,' she remarked when it was done.

Howard was tempted to tell her 'You always say that',

but managed to hold his tongue.

Their evenings were mostly boring, and this one was more boring than usual. They were each glad to go to bed, to their separate rooms. Officially, the issue was Howard's snoring. Unspoken but acknowledged by both, the matter ran deeper than that.

In their attempts to have a child years ago, they had put themselves through torment. IVF and surrogacy came too late for them, but they tried every imaginable position, time of day, time of the month and foodstuff.

'Excuse me, we must go upstairs to fuck. We're trying for a baby, you know,' they almost told visitors on several occasions.

The fruit of all this effort was two painful miscarriages, one of them very late term. Sex = pain = no result. After this, Cynthia continued to go through the motions, but she rarely found any interest much less enjoyment in sex. Their intimate life dwindled away until it disappeared.

The last occasion, ten years ago, had been an abject failure when Howard was unable to rise to his duty. He kept at his work, however. His fingers at least were reliably rigid.

'Howard, stop fiddling around,' Cynthia said witheringly.

'I'm sorry, Cyn,' he replied pulling his hand away. 'It doesn't get easier as we grow old. There's this Viagra stuff we read about. It might be worth a try ...'

'Don't worry about it. Go to sleep. It doesn't matter.' And she meant it. Soon after that, with little spoken about it, they took to their separate beds.

Now Howard lay on his bed and thought about his marriage. They were within sight of their fiftieth anniversary, the golden one – heaven help us! He was fond of her after a fashion, yet had he ever loved her? He had supposed so back in the day. Now he saw that he had married her on the rebound from Meg Denby. She had been there before Meg and she was there after Meg.

Why Cynthia married Howard was more of a puzzle. She was in her upper twenties, which was late to be unpartnered in their circle in those days. He supposed she had seen in him a coming man. Certainly he hadn't remained trapped in Bristol as most of their set had done. Cynthia didn't want much from life, but she wanted to be able to play her tennis, pursue her hobbies and live in a house that would hold its own to all-comers. He had fulfilled that side of the bargain. He had risen steadily through the ranks at the *Messenger*, becoming editor and then upon his retirement chairman of the board. She was Lady Jenkins. The houses meanwhile became steadily grander until their present destination of the Snelgroves' mansion.

Cynthia had proved a good wife in every respect. His work as editor and now chairman meant a great deal of socialising at public events. Cynthia carried off these occasions in style. She had been quite a pretty girl, although the sort that looked better in shorts whacking some sort of ball rather than a ball gown. She had matured into a presentable woman. Not much of this was left now. Poor Cynthia had become dumpy. She no longer troubled much about her clothes except when she was dolled up for official occasions as the chairman's wife. She had trouble with her legs and was on statins.

Howard was aware that he was in no better a place. Originally hovering around six feet tall, he had shrunk by an inch if not more. He had the sort of figure that no amount of official dinners could bloat or expand, but his lean appearance now inclined to the cadaverous. Great folds of skin covered his neck and upper arms where once had been firm flesh. He had trouble with his knees and other ailments working upwards.

At least they were in the same boat physically. Their marriage had never been a grand passion. Rather, it was a comfortable partnership. The pictures in their photo albums told the story. At official occasions they not unnaturally looked rather formal, but at social events like the tennis club dance or when meeting friends, even in the wedding photos, they looked content enough – but where was the joy? No shots were to be found where they were lit up with happiness. What a contrast with his few pictures with Meg! Cynthia didn't know about these. Diplomatically, she had never asked. The pictures were mainly taken at Lowmere Abbey, Meg's home, or at film industry functions. She has the composed smile of the professional actress, but his face is irradiated with joy. Howard's body language, frozen in time at 1/60th of a second, says 'Look at me, life is good!'

Howard had never been tempted to stray. Numerous pretty, sexy girl reporters had passed through his hands (figuratively speaking), but nest-fouling would have been risky in the provincial puritanism of the *Messenger*. The city as a whole, where he was a figure of consequence, was another matter. After Meg, though, no girl could measure up. None seemed worth it.

The fact was he and Cynthia needed each other. Both were only children so there were no siblings to lean on. They weren't close to their respective cousins. It would be a lonely life for whoever was left.

Even now, with their sex life long over, Howard sometimes yearned for the creak of the bedroom door opening

– no knock, of course – and Cynthia would be with him. It wasn't going to happen. He could slip into her room, but he knew the response that would get.

By the time he'd worked through these thoughts, sleep was destroyed. He lay awake, dreading the alarm at seven o'clock in readiness for his drive to the office. Sometimes he asked himself why he was putting himself through this routine. He well knew the answer: if he didn't go to the office what else would he do all day?

# TWO

THE chairman was in his office working through documents for a board meeting when he was interrupted by Marcia, the secretary whom he shared with the editor. Sir Roger Hudson, one of the local magnates, had phoned and left Howard a message. No, Sir Roger hadn't asked to be put through; in fact, he had insisted on not being put through.

'The message,' said Marcia, 'is that if Sir Howard would like to call on him at four this afternoon he has some news to impart that he believes will be of interest to the *Messenger*.'

Howard's first thought was, Why me? One would not normally approach the chairman of the company with a story, which he presumed this was. His second thought was to be regrettably detained elsewhere and to send a reporter. He didn't see why he should be summoned at Sir Roger's pleasure on a moment's notice. Then curiosity trumped his irritation. He decided to go.

Howard and Sir Roger had spent the better part of fifty years circling each other. In all that time they had hardly spoken. They had disliked each other on sight, at that first occasion when Roger came with Meg to the party at Mrs Snelgrove's and Howard was there gathering morsels for the gossip column. Before that, Roger had complained about an item soon after he had inherited the baronetcy where Howard had accidentally called him 'Mr Hudson' in print.

It was all so long ago and so trivial, yet those vibrations resonated down the years. Howard thought Roger was a caricature of a pompous Edwardian hunting squire. Roger no doubt returned the compliment by seeing Howard as a provincial nonentity who ought to pursue his lowly trade in a grubby mac. And now Sir Roger was asking to see him of all people. Why? There was only one way to find out.

Grawton Hall, Sir Roger's home, was an Elizabethan gem – a fortified manor house of good Yorkshire stone built at a time when turrets and crenellations were for ornamentation rather than serious defence. Its estate of two and a half thousand acres marched alongside the Lowmere Abbey estate, Meg's home. Unlike Lowmere, Grawton wasn't open to the public. Howard had never seen inside it. Sir Roger, a bachelor, was sociable, but his circle didn't include *Messenger* people even at the highest level.

Howard rang the door bell, which jangled in the distance. He heard footsteps padding towards him. A woman in late middle age, perhaps the housekeeper, appeared. She was neither friendly nor unfriendly.

'Yes, sir?' she said expressionlessly.

'Howard Jenkins to see Sir Roger. He's expecting me.'

'He is, sir. This way please.'

If Howard expected Roger to live in single squalor, he was off the mark. The place appeared spotless. They walked through the great hall where ancestors looked down from freshly painted walls on furniture that shone from constant waxing. Silverware and china glittered in the sunlight pouring through stained glass windows.

He was shown into a comfortably furnished smaller sitting room where Roger Hudson was waiting. Howard saw among the family photos scattered around tables and ledges a shot of Roger and Meg. They were at some party. Meg looked happy in that girl-next-door way that had carried her through major British pictures to Hollywood, her hair cascading on to her shoulders as ever. Roger, an arm clutched round her waist, looked the proud possessor. Howard looked away quickly, hoping Roger hadn't noticed.

Roger Hudson was a bear of a man, still powerful in his mid-seventies but with the first suggestions of fragility to come. His manner, too, was neither friendly nor unfriendly.

'Thank you for coming, Sir Howard,' he said. No words of welcome or apology for the late notice.

'Very happy to do so,' Howard responded, then to cover the silence when Roger said nothing more he went on: 'What a beautiful home you have!' Realising this could be taken as a half-a-crown tourist's comment on the house itself, he added hastily: 'Everything is so spick and span.'

'Nothing to do with me,' said Roger. 'Mrs Matthews here, my housekeeper, takes the credit for that.'

She put her inscrutability aside at that. 'Thank you very much, sir,' she said. 'I do my best.'

'Thank *you*, Mrs Matthews,' said Roger, which she correctly took as the signal to leave them.

'Some tea, sir?'

'Perhaps later.'

Howard meanwhile wondered why he was sitting there. He assumed that Roger had some story to offer, but why hadn't he asked for a reporter or at least the editor of the newspaper? Why the chairman of the board? Was it some devious payback by calling attention to his former lowly role as a gossip reporter? He could hear Cynthia saying, 'Don't be so paranoid!' His wife was right. The answer was straightforward.

Without any niceties, Roger came straight to the point. 'I asked for you personally because I have important news that I want to publish in the *Messenger* alone, and I want it to be accurate,' he said.

'You may be sure of that.'

'I don't know any *Messenger* people,' Roger continued, 'but under your leadership it has always had a reputation for accuracy. I assume that apart from one unfortunate episode many years ago you are yourself an accurate reporter.'

This was a reference to the 'Mr Hudson' incident. Across almost half a century, Howard remembered it only too well. He was the *Messenger's* diary or gossip column reporter. It was the first time he encountered Meg Denby. The event was a literary lunch. Meg was with Roger, and Howard had written in the flip gossip column style:

> Miss Denby talked of wining and dining with Mr Roger Hudson, a farmer. Then Mr Hudson proposed a visit to the bookstall. Food for thought? Clearly, he is not a man to live by bread alone.

After that Howard began to pursue Meg, that impossibly beautiful and delightful girl. He obtained a phone number that he feared was Roger's. As it turned out to be. Roger answered the phone and declared there had been a 'serious mistake' in the diary item.

Howard wondered whether Sir Roger had taken offence at the blasphemous reference to bread. But it wasn't the bread.

'A most serious mistake,' Roger repeated. 'Most embarrassing. One must admit that the William Hazlitt column is widely read. I'm the last person to stand on ceremony' – which was untrue – 'but the fact is that last

October I inherited the baronetcy from my uncle, Sir Lewis Hudson.'

Sir Roger was still grumbling when he grudgingly put Meg on the line.

'Good morning to you, Howard,' she said cheerfully.

He noted the easy use of his first name.

'I was just phoning to ask you if you thought the bit about yourself was all right,' he began tentatively. 'I mean, you didn't mind it?'

'Since when has an actress minded bits about herself in the paper?' she laughed. 'It was a very nice thing to write, Howard, and thank you very much. Do you always make a point of phoning your victims, and asking them if they approve?' There was a hint a mischief in her voice.

'Well, no. I simply thought I – I – I reckoned I should after what Sir Roger had said about no quotes. It wasn't a quote, you see, it was a comment.'

'That's quite all right.'

'I'm afraid Sir Roger is upset about me referring to him as Mr Hudson.'

Meg, whose father was a viscount and who had been around titles all her life, laughed again. 'He's just being stuffy,' she said. 'I told him that the only bad publicity is no publicity.'

Howard had never forgotten the incident. Nor, clearly, had Roger. Amazing that it still rankled.

What was he saying? 'I assume you are yourself an accurate reporter.'

'I believe so,' said Howard modestly.

'Well then, the news I have to give the *Messenger* is that I've decided to sell Grawton.'

This was a shock. No rumours were circulating to this

effect so far as Howard knew. Roger looked on silently, almost challenging him to be astonished.

'This is most unexpected, Sir Roger,' Howard managed eventually. 'May I ask why?'

'Simple,' the other responded. 'No direct heirs. No one in the family I want to leave it to. The closest relation is a cousin, Nigel Hudson. He lives in the Virgin Islands and is a financial adviser specialising in tax evasion. Not that he'd put it like that, of course. He'll inherit the title. I can't do anything about that, but I can do something about the estate. It's in my sole control – no trust controlling it, no entail. And he shan't have it.'

'You're keen for your cousin not to inherit the estate then?'

'Absolutely not! Never had any time for the fellow. A stuck-up ass. He's made clear – clearer than he should have from his point of view – that he has no interest in the estate. The first thing he'd do is sell it. Well, I'd sooner sell it myself and get the financial benefits.'

The sale of the Grawton estate was big news for the *Messenger* with its readership of gentry and gentry dreamers and wannabees. Howard wished he'd brought a reporter's notebook or even an audio recorder. It was a long time since he'd handled either. The best he could do was a pocket jotter, which he now brought out.

'You don't mind if I jot down some facts?'

'That's what you're here for,' Sir Roger answered as if he were preparing a temporary secretary to take dictation.

'I understand your point that the title and the estate don't have to go together,' said Howard. 'So is there no one else you'd like to leave the estate to?'

'Yes, plenty. A hedge-fund billionaire, an oil sheikh,

a Russian kleptocrat – all would do nicely. They would eat up the atmosphere and the status of an English country estate.

'Particularly the hunting and shooting,' Roger went on. 'There's no money in farming these days. Hunting and shooting are another story. They are the very stamp of the country gentleman, and that's what they're after.'

'I was thinking of something nearer home. The National Trust, for example?'

'The National Trust? Pah! Some little squirt came to see Grawton, and said too much as far as I was concerned ... explained how they'd present the house in its period of greatest glories. I wasn't playing that game. I want to hand on a home in the here and now, not a shrine to history.'

'Or Lowmere Abbey?' Howard pursued. 'You share a boundary. Would Lord Chilcott be interested to augment his land with yours?'

'Jeremy? Not a scrap of it! He couldn't get anywhere near the price. He struggles to keep his roofs watertight.'

Roger's manner signalled that he was tired of this line of questioning. 'Believe me, I've looked at every possibility. A sale to a rich foreigner is the best way.'

'What will you do, Sir Roger?'

'Go and live in Madeira,' Roger replied firmly. 'I have a house there, and I like the idea of spending my last years there. No money worries, year-round sun more or less, cheap booze. This climate doesn't do when one's in one's seventies. And my hunting days are almost over. My knees and back won't take many more jumps.'

'I have much the same problem,' said Howard.

Roger registered this with a flicker until he remembered who he was talking to. But Howard was keen to capitalise on this glimpse of the personal.

'Look, we've known each other for a long time. Can't we drop the "Sir Roger" and the "Sir Howard"? I'm "Howard".'

'Known *of* each other for a long time,' Roger corrected. 'And I think it's more appropriate to stay as we are.'

Very well, thought Howard, if I'm to be the hack I'll ask a hack's question.

'How do you feel about Grawton passing out of family control after three hundred years?'

Continuing the line was a preoccupation of landed families. Nobody wanted to be the one to give it up. The Hudsons had been settled at Grawton since the early eighteenth century when John Hudson, an ambitious sheep farmer, took advantage of the burgeoning wave of enclosures to put together a small estate, soon following this with a baronetcy. The estate grew by degrees to reach its fullest extent in Victorian times. The family was more successful than many in hanging on to land so that, creditably, two and a half thousand acres, or around half the previous amount, remained.

Perhaps, however, the Hudsons felt less strongly than many about continuing the line. Their history included several cousin inheritances. In one case the husband changed his name to Hudson upon marrying the Hudson heiress. Sir Roger had inherited from another bachelor, his Uncle Lewis.

Roger showed no sign of being disturbed by the question, nor was he disposed to answer it at any personal level. 'If circumstances had been different it would be good to hand on to a son or even a daughter, but as things are I believe my course is the best' was all he said.

Both men – Howard as childless as Roger – knew

what he was referring to. The shadow of Meg Denby continued to fall between them.

Howard asked some questions of detail about the proposed sale until he had enough to go to print with. It was late in the afternoon and therefore well into the *Messenger's* daily production cycle. The story must run tomorrow to stay ahead of the pack. There was no time for a photographer to get out to Grawton. They would have to rely on file pictures plus a snap of Sir Roger that Howard took on his smartphone.

Roger made no attempt to delay Howard. He never had the tea that Mrs Matthews suggested, nor – as wine o'clock came into view – 'something stronger'. Howard left the house feeling like a tradesman, but with an exclusive literally in his pocket. As soon as he was out of sight of the house, he pulled the car over and phoned the editor. It was agreed that space would be left in next day's paper for a story and picture on page one, turning to more content (words and pictures) on an inside page.

# THREE

THE features editor was in charge of the gossip column, now named simply Hazlitt. He came up to Howard in the staff restaurant looking as excited as a middle-aged, office-bound journalist ever did. 'Got a cracking story for the column,' he announced. 'Howard, you have connections with Lowmere Abbey, don't you?'

'Had,' said Howard.

'Whatever. I just heard that Benjamin, Meg Denby's son and Lord Chilcott's nephew, has come from Italy on a visit for the first time in twenty years. Estrangement over. Kissed and made up, it seems.'

It was a strong social story for the *Messenger* and the news media more widely.

'Let's get it first,' the features editor continued. 'Fortunately, the Chilcotts aren't publicity seekers – quite the opposite, in fact – so we should have it to ourselves for a bit. We can go big on this. I'll send Emily. As well as being very able, she can charm young Benjamin.'

'Young Benjamin is within sight of fifty ...'

'All the more susceptible then! And he is Italian, more or less.'

Howard sensed that something was about to be asked of him. He was right.

'I don't suppose you could find the time to go with Emily and oil the wheels with Benjamin?' ' said the features editor.

Howard readily agreed. He was curious and in truth he had plenty of time. As he admitted to himself, he had turned the chairman's job, needing one day a week, into a full-time occupation in order to get out of the house. A late start to the day, an early finish and in between, lunch at the club took care of the other four days. An agreeable routine.

He had followed Benjamin's life so far as he could from his birth. One look proclaimed that Ben was the son of that erstwhile golden couple, Meg Denby and the now-forgotten heartthrob actor Everard Hughes. The wonderfully symmetrical, oval face proclaimed Meg, but the boy took most of his looks from Everard. The height, the long blond hair and the swagger that comes naturally to many very tall people.

Benjamin's story, Howard felt, was a sad one despite his advantages of looks and background. He spent his first years at Lowmere Abbey, brought up by his grandparents but mainly by his Italian nanny, Julia. Ben's mother meanwhile convinced herself that with her filmmaking and travelling commitments it was for the best for Ben to be at Lowmere.

'Besides, London is not a healthy place to bring up a child,' she would say.

Everard, the father, had never been able to summon much interest in Benjamin. For the short time he was with Meg he was happy to go along with the arrangement.

Lord and Lady Chilcott were kind enough within the constraints of the aristocratic conventions of child-rearing and their own active lives. Most of the time, however, Ben was with Julia. He developed a strong attachment to the nanny. He made a good show of indifference to his mother.

Jeremy, Meg's elder brother, told Howard there had been fearful rows in the house as the boy acquired Italian as his first language. Meg came home one day to find Ben and Julia playing with bricks. Ben, twelve months old, threw a tantrum as his mother took him into his arms and kissed and cuddled him. Eventually Meg put him down. 'Mamma,' he wailed, looking straight at Julia. At that moment Montmorency, a shabby cat of mixed parentage, jumped into the nursery through an open window. 'Gatto,' exclaimed a delighted Ben.

'Was that Italian?' Meg asked incredulously, hoping she had misheard. Julia, of course, denied that she was talking to Ben only in Italian. But the matter was soon put beyond doubt. Pointing to a rubber ball, Ben had announced, 'Palla!' He then indicated a Lego house and declared, 'Casa!'

Jeremy was in the room when Meg let rip at their mother. 'How could you let Julia speak to Ben in Italian?' she demanded.

'I expect she uses English as well, darling,' said Lady Chilcott. 'I'm sure Ben will grow out of his Italian when he leaves the nursery.'

Meg protested: 'I don't want Ben growing up confused. I think Julia should be replaced.'

Lady Chilcott responded that good live-in nannies were almost impossible to find these days, and if Meg were that unhappy she'd have to look after Ben herself. 'I may have to start doing that despite my work and everything,' said Meg. Even as she said it she knew it wouldn't happen, couldn't happen.

Ben resolutely refused to go to preparatory school. Eventually Meg gave way. The boy stayed at Lowmere with Julia until he left for Eton aged fourteen. By then each had become bilingual. The Denbys noticed that Ben was more comfortable in Italian. Most annoyingly for the rest of the household, the pair had a private language they could use whenever they wished. Julia returned to Italy. For his university education the young man chose to go to Italy, to the University of Padua. This was the city where Julia was living. And it was where he had been ever since, with Julia as his stand-in mother.

Ben picked up a living in a succession of jobs all with some cultural character – he ran a bookshop, opened a restaurant, became a painter, a novelist, a poet. None of these activities lasted long or was attended with great success, but he was understood to be happy enough. With his striking looks and as Meg Denby's son, he readily picked up work as an extra or bit part player in Italian pictures. It never progressed to substantial roles. 'Doesn't want it enough' was the word around the film lots. He was not thought to be married or to have been married.

While Benjamin was estranged from his mother, he had no quarrel with the rest of the Denbys. He often spoke about happy times at Lowmere Abbey, where he grew up, but his visits became ever rarer until they stopped altogether. Now he was back and, in a message through his uncle Jeremy, was happy to talk to the *Messenger*.

'Benjamin will speak to you on one condition. It is that you don't ask about or refer to his mother,' Lord Chilcott told Emily Stimson, the reporter.

'May I ask why?'

'I simply don't know. He feels strongly about it. Believe me, he'll stop the interview if you ignore the condition.'

Emily had to agree to the condition, but she grumbled to Howard as they drove over to Lowmere: 'What are we doing here, Sir Howard ...?'

'Please, "Howard" will do ...'

'Thank you,' said Emily. "But how are we supposed to write this piece without its main raison d'etre?'

'*Hamlet* without mentioning the Prince of Denmark,' said Howard, who had a cliché for most occasions.

'Buckingham Palace without mentioning the Queen of England,' Emily responded.

They both giggled. As Emily drove with her attention fixed on the road, Howard had ample opportunity to admire her long legs, shapely thighs and taut breasts, shown to advantage by her tight-cut trousers and jumper. Everything was so much more exciting with trousers and jeans than with dresses, he thought, even if he was too old, too tired and too absorbed in his memories to do anything about it.

'We can't ask about Meg, but nothing can stop you writing her into the article as background – lots of it,' he said.

'Awesome,' Emily responded.

'So why did Meg and Benjamin fall out?' she asked.

'It goes back to earliest childhood, I think,' said Howard. 'I suppose Ben thought Meg didn't give him the support she should have. He saw very little of his mother as a child. She was always away filming or working on her causes. To make it worse, the father – Everard Hughes – didn't want to know. Ben was brought up at Lowmere by his grandparents and the nanny, Julia. That's why she's now Zia Julia – Aunt Julia – and Ben lives in Italy.'

He added: 'It's very sad. I'm sure Meg thought that with her commitments and Everard having deserted her she was doing it for the best.' Even now he couldn't help defending her.

Lowmere Abbey was invisible from the public road. It was some time along the drive before the house revealed itself – a long building of three storeys in severe, grey Yorkshire stone. It still managed to feel more like a home than a barracks. The mansion had been built from the stones of the demolished abbey after which it was named. The chancel of the monks' church had been incorporated into the house to make the family's private chapel. The eighteenth-century park swept up to the house at the front and back while to one side was the Victorian legacy of a magnificent herbaceous border.

'Wow!' said Emily.

They were shown into the library at Lowmere – a room Howard remembered well. Nothing seemed to have changed in almost fifty years. That went for the books too, he reckoned. Any modern books the Chilcotts possessed must be housed elsewhere.

'I'll leave you to it,' Jeremy said to Benjamin. 'I'm sure you don't need me to hold your hand.'

Howard noticed a flicker of puzzlement from Ben. 'Ah, I see. You don't need to stay with me. No, of course not, uncle.'

These few words told Howard that Ben was fluent enough in English although he wouldn't necessarily know every expression. He spoke with a slightly clipped accent.

Benjamin Hughes – he had taken his father's name even though his parents never married – as he approached fifty was a carbon copy of Everard in his later years, before illness and a life of excess destroyed his looks. Ben had the same height, hair and above all the languid, confident manner of the late movie idol. He was clearly in excellent shape.

'Please sit down,' he said while draping himself over the arm of a chair. 'I will help you in any way I can for your article.'

Howard was conscious of not upstaging Emily. He gestured to the reporter to put the first question

'Thank you for seeing us, Mr Hughes,' Emily began decorously. 'I believe it's many years since you were at Lowmere. What's it feel like to be back?'

Ben expressed his pleasure at being back, was happy to find so little had changed, wanted to catch up with his family (he didn't specify whom), was sorry that his grandparents had passed on, didn't know how long he would be staying, had nothing surprising to say about his life in Italy and had no special plans about things to do while he was here. Above all, he didn't mention his mother.

The interview wasn't yielding much despite Emily's best efforts.

'Hunting and shooting are big activities here, as you know,' Howard put in. 'Are you planning some of that perhaps?'

Ben was not. It was so many years since he'd ridden or handled a gun he supposed he'd forgotten how. Another line closed down. Then, with visions of a dull article before them, Emily and Howard's luck changed.

'Can you suggest a nice village close to a town,' Ben asked. 'I have been away so long I have forgotten all the places,' he added for explanation.

'In what way, nice?' Howard replied.

Ben explained that he meant a place with lots of character – traditional cottages as well as a 'ristorante' and other facilities. It needed to be both rural and close to a town.

'Are you looking for a cottage?' Emily asked with surprise.

Ben agreed that he might be. 'Zia Julia, the lady who brought me up, is dying,' he said. 'When she is gone, perhaps it will be time to come home. England is much changed but here at Lowmere, not so much.'

Howard and Emily named several villages that might be suitable. Emily gestured to Howard to look at her open notebook. She had scrawled: 'LETS GO BEFORE HE PUTS THIS STUFF OFF RECORD!!!' Between them they brought the interview quickly to a close.

Throughout the meeting Ben and Howard had dealt with each other as the strangers they were. Howard had been aware of Ben from birth minus nine months (give or take), had glimpsed him once or twice over the years but had never spoken to him; the younger man gave no sign that he knew of any connection between Howard and Meg. Now he turned to Howard and asked: 'May I have a private word, Sir Howard?'

'This is Emily's interview, Mr Hughes.'

'It is a matter for men,' Ben continued.

'We don't make that distinction in journalism any more,' said Howard, who was happy to be able to show Emily his equality credentials.

'It doesn't matter at all,' said Emily, ready to put her feminism aside.

Lord Chilcott, who was hovering in the background, had no problem entertaining an attractive woman. 'If you're all right with it, Miss Stimson, why don't I arrange coffee for us, and the others can talk in the garden?'

Ben and Howard stepped out on to the terrace. Even at Lowmere some things must change in half a century.

Howard saw that the park looked subtly different. Younger trees had become taller, denser. Here and there were gaps where mature trees had died.

'This place must be full of memories for you,' he said to Ben as an ice-breaker.

'And for you, I think,' the younger man replied. So Ben knew.

Howard said nothing, but made an almost imperceptible nod in acknowledgement.

'Sir Howard, I think you knew my father,' Ben continued. 'What was he like? I have no memories of him.'

How to play this question?! Howard could hardly tell the son that Everard was a selfish chancer. 'He was a huge film star in his day,' he began cautiously. 'He looked very like you, Ben. He was one of the most dashing men in England.'

Ben looked puzzled.

'Handsome and popular ...' Howard explained. 'All the women adored him.'

'But he did not adore them. I know he was gay. And he died of Aids.'

Howard said: 'Yes he did. I think he adored women in his way. He adored your mother until a man called Jason came along.' There, he'd said it! How could he have this conversation without mentioning Meg? Ben didn't respond. 'But he was probably confused about his sexual identity.'

'"Sexual identity"? Ah yes. Sir Howard, I'm not confused about my sexual identity.'

'Of course not.'

'I mean, like my father I also am gay.'

Ben had Everard's looks, but he was clearly a more genuine character. He must have got that from Meg.

Howard couldn't help thinking of all the girls who would be disappointed. He simply said: 'It's not an issue for me, Ben, or for almost everybody else these days.'

'Sir Howard, what do you think about changing sex?'

Omigod, where did that come from! Is Ben about to announce that he's to become a woman? 'That's a very big question,' Howard said, 'which I'm not qualified to answer. I'm not a doctor or a psychiatrist. You have to remember that it's a new idea for most people. I'd say that many people find it more difficult than homosexuality.'

'In Italy too,' said Ben. 'What I told you about Zia Julia is true. She is dying. But there is more. My partner Guido was born a woman. He is going through the er- procedures now.'

Howard knew the best thing to say was nothing.

'In Italy we find much hostility. I think England will be better for us. Do you agree, Sir Howard?'

'I do so far as England is concerned. Whatever they may think, English people tend to keep their feelings to themselves. And it may be, if it follows the course of so many other social changes we oldsters ...

'... old people have got used to, changing sex will seem entirely usual in ten years' time.' Privately, he wondered whether it would be so, or would it be seen as a fashion that passed.

Ben looked relieved. 'I shall spend my time at Lowmere looking for a house. For me a city would be a better place. However, Guido is a "country boy". It is one of the few subjects where we don't agree.'

Howard thanked Ben for sharing this deeply private information. 'None of this need appear in the article,' he said. 'Aunt Julia is the reason you're returning. I'll keep your secret, Ben.'

Emily and Howard's visit to Lowmere produced a lacklustre article for the Hazlitt column. The main point of interest was that Lord Chilcott's nephew, Meg Denby's son, was house-hunting in the area after decades living in Italy. The next day they were greeted with a headline in the *Sun*:

## PEER'S NEPHEW HAS SEX CHANGE BOYFRIEND

The *Messenger* editor, Rob Willis, was furious. He rarely swore, but he did so now. 'Christ, how did we miss that!'

'It's not really a *Messenger* story, is it, Rob?' said Howard. 'It's more of a mass market story.'

'For fuck's sake, Howard, with our dropping circulation every story's a *Messenger* story! There's no mass market and up-market anymore.'

'It wasn't a line we were going with,' Emily put in, unwisely.

'Hell, then it should have been, young lady.' The editor's gender sensitivity had deserted him under stress. 'Don't they teach human interest in journalism schools these days? Did you ask about his marital status?'

Emily was silent. Howard felt the need to rescue a damsel in distress. 'Benjamin told me when he and I were alone. I said we would respect this deeply private matter.'

Willis groaned. 'If I had any hair I'd pull it out now!'

Howard, the chairman of the board, was angry at being publicly upbraided, but if one acts as a reporter one must expect to be treated as a reporter.

'Am I right,' Willis continued, 'Benjamin didn't put it off the record but we did? Our job as journalists is to find things out and print them, not sit on them! With all due respect, Howard, have you been in management too long?'

# FOUR

THANKS to the complete personnel records, the exact day was known when Howard joined the *Messenger* in 1963. On the fiftieth anniversary the commemorative article appeared with a picture spread of the man through the years and messages of congratulation from the great and the good of the county from the lord lieutenant downwards. Willis, the editor, had played it big, Howard's lapse over Ben and his transgender partner being long forgotten.

The article began with the predictability of a heron gobbling a goldfish:

> "I'm as excited to be working at the *Messenger* now as I was when I started here fifty years ago." In these words chairman of the board Sir Howard Jenkins reflected on his record service with the newspaper.

The article jogged along in a predictable way. The challenges of the digital age and the lavatory redecorated for the Queen were included; there was nothing about the Pill and how the Sixties revealed girls' legs for the first time. It was the sort of article that Howard had seen a hundred times before, had himself written often enough, and it was exactly what was needed.

'Excellent article, Howard!' said friends and well-wishers.

Howard found himself giving interviews for local TV and radio in which he said all the same things in different words.

On the anniversary day the company hosted a reception, dinner and dance in the biggest ballroom in the city, attended by the region's finest (or at least the most prominent). It was black tie for men and full-length gowns for women. Rob Willis was present. A dinner would be held later for the rest of the *Messenger* staff.

Cynthia, who came to life on the big occasions, seemed to have shed a decade as she chatted animatedly to the guests crowding around her.

'Even all those years ago in Bristol I knew he was heading for the top,' she was heard to say. Or: 'Sometimes I wish he would take it easier at his age. He doesn't know the meaning of the word "retirement".' Or: 'If he cuts himself I look for printer's ink not blood!'

Howard, circulating, found Jeremy Chilcott and his wife. Benjamin was not to be seen. Sir Roger Hudson was another absentee.

'I hope Ben doesn't blame me for his secret coming out in the *Sun*,' Howard said to Lord Chilcott. The Chilcotts didn't appear to notice the accidental double entendre.

'I don't think it even crossed his mind,' Jeremy replied. 'The news leaked out in the Italian press, and he assumes the *Sun* got it from there.'

'Even so it's a pity he isn't here so I could tell him myself.'

'Not a chance!' said Lord Chilcott. 'He spends hours every evening on the phone to Italy. Not my bill fortunately. He uses Skype. It's always this Guido fellow, woman, whatever we're talking about.'

'Jeremy, you can't say things like that these days!' Lady Chilcott exclaimed.

'I just did. It doesn't matter a jot to me, but Lowmere village isn't ready for that sort of thing. It's as well Benjamin is looking for a house nearer town.'

'I think Ben's a lovely boy,' Lady Chilcott declared. 'I don't care about his er-orientation.'

'Whatever you say, dear. Look, the lord lieutenant's over there. Let's get a word with him.'

At dinner Howard, as the guest of honour, sat with the lord lieutenant on his right and Lord Chilcott on his left. His mind went back almost fifty years to another top table in this very room. This was when from his lowly seat at the reporters' table he first saw a gorgeous, mysterious girl just three places away from where he sat now. It was Meg Denby.

Concentrate! The lord lieutenant was on his feet.

'I shan't keep you long,' said the Queen's representative. 'I know you're keen to get on with the merriment.' This was an allusion to the dancing – or was it the drinking? 'I'm only too pleased – honoured in fact – to have the opportunity of paying tribute to Sir Howard for his fifty years of devoted service to this newspaper, this city and this county [loud applause and cries of "hear, hear"]. Starting as a junior reporter in 1963 – and as someone the same age as Howard I hope he'll forgive me for saying that this sometimes seems like the Palaeolithic Era [laughter, smiling acknowledgement from the guest of honour] – Howard progressed steadily through the ranks until he became the editor, where he served for twenty-five exceptional years [applause]. Twelve-hour days were the norm for Howard for six days, sometimes seven every week. From the morning editorial conference at 10am to the first edition going to print at 10pm – you see I've been initiated into the secrets of the journalistic day [laughter] – the editor was there, hands-on [applause]. Thanks to the editor's devotion to duty [more applause] and the support of his lovely wife Cynthia [loud applause] a great newspaper has become even greater [fervent applause].'

The lord lieutenant was understandably pleased at the response to his speech. He was on a roll. The promised brevity of his remarks looked uncertain. He continued:

'As a reporter Howard covered most of the big events of the period.' He listed a number of them, most of which Howard hadn't covered, but who cared? 'Howard is also an easy colleague to work with [true]. He is noted for his sense of humour [untrue]. Unlike Howard I can't do jokes [respectively untrue and true], but I want to tell you about one of the smaller stories Howard covered. This was a court case where a man was convicted of vandalism. He had painted in huge letters on the door of York Minster "To hell with the Pope!" (Please excuse my language, ladies and gentlemen.) Now York Minster is of course an Anglican cathedral and not a Catholic one. So the judge asked him why he had painted "To hell with the Pope!" "Simple," the man replied. "Because 'To hell with the Archbishops of York and Canterbury!' wouldn't fit on the door [slight delay followed by moderate laughter]".'

If the lord lieutenant had ended there, proposed the health of Sir Howard coupled with that of Lady Jenkins and sat down, it would have been remembered as a pleasant and appropriate speech. Unfortunately, he laboured on for another ten minutes. Howard gave a short reply; then finally, with relief, the guests could start the dancing and the serious drinking.

'Thank you for that, Howie,' said Cynthia when it was done and they were back home. 'I don't know when I enjoyed myself so much.'

'On to the next anniversary!' he replied lightly, putting a hand round her waist and squeezing slightly. But she pulled away.

After the excitements of the fiftieth, life resumed its placid course for Howard. The sometimes frenzied atmosphere of daily production didn't reach into his spacious office. As chairman he was concerned with broader issues. The *Messenger* in common with newspapers all over the country was struggling with falling circulation. Older readers died off and younger people saw no reason to buy a paper when they could read the same content free on the internet. Head office, sarcastically known as 'Corporate HQ', was often on his back demanding ever more economies. HQ in turn had restive shareholders on its back.

'Just be glad we're not in an industry that makes proper money ... then we'd really have activist investors to contend with!' the business editor commented.

These issues were rarely pressing enough to trouble Howard's daily routine. One day, however, he returned from lunch at the club to find a message that promised something of interest.

'A Mr Nigel Hudson wants to make an appointment to see you,' Marcia announced. 'He just said it was about Grawton.'

It was quickly confirmed that Nigel Hudson was the cousin that Sir Roger had spoken of, the heir to the baronetcy. A meeting was set for the next morning.

The man in question was unmistakeably a Hudson – a big man and a younger, better dressed version of Roger. He looked well preserved late fifties. Howard pictured him going to the gym daily, sweating over weights, exercise bikes and treadmills. Nigel had perfectly coiffed hair and wore a suit with the sheen of high quality. His tie was that of a top school, which he had doubtless actually attended.

His first action was to thrust a card into Howard's hand, following this up with a firm but not too firm handshake. The card announced him as an investment consultant and chartered accountant based in the British Virgin Islands. Howard, who disliked the man on sight, had no difficulty seeing him as an expert in tax evasion, as Roger had said.

'Thank you for seeing me, Sir Howard,' he began pleasantly. 'Happy to do so,' replied an equally pleasant Howard. 'What brings you to Yorkshire from the Virgin Islands, Mr Hudson?'

'Yes indeed ... let's get straight to the point. I'm here on Grawton business.' Nigel produced a newspaper cutting from his pocket. 'I've seen your article. Cousin Roger didn't give you the full story. There's more to be said and I'm here to say it.'

'This is really a matter for a reporter. I'll ask Emily Stimson to come in. I only wrote that article because of my long association with Sir Roger Hudson.'

'You still have that long association with Cousin Roger,' the other observed logically. 'It's you I want. I always deal with the man at the top.'

Howard was on the edge of saying these weren't business dealings so far as he was concerned. He was privately pleased at the chance of writing another story. He simply said: 'Very well. Please speak to me and we'll take it from there.'

Nigel settled himself in the practised way he adopted for a sales pitch, adjusting one of his trouser legs so the crease fell perfectly.

'It's no secret that Cousin Roger and I don't get along,' he said. 'He could have been like an uncle to me when I was growing up. He wasn't. I might have been the tiresome son of one of his tenants for all the friendliness he showed me. He has no direct heir, as you correctly pointed out in the article. I'm the heir to his title. He can't prevent that – he would if he could! – but he's told the world that he's selling the estate. I'm here to stop that.'

'What do you mean?'

'I mean simply that I'll inherit both the title and the estate. He can't stop it.'

'I understand that Sir Roger is the outright owner of the Grawton estate. There's no trust and no entail. Are you disputing that?' said Howard.

'I'm not. He owns it outright. What he can't do is sell it because a contract already exists to pass it on to me when the time comes.'

This was a totally unexpected development. Nigel looked pleased at the shock his announcement had produced.

'A contract? Sir Roger said nothing about a contract,' Howard managed eventually.

'He wouldn't. He'd prefer to forget it. He's not ga-ga ... he remembers it all right.'

'What would be the point in pretending it doesn't exist? It can be produced at any time.'

Nigel didn't miss a beat as he continued smoothly: 'This contract is a verbal one, sworn before a witness.' So the matter wasn't as cut and dried as it had seemed.

'Who's the witness?'

'My cousin Sir Lewis Hudson. He forced Roger to

agree to keep both estate and title in the family.'

'But Sir Lewis has been dead for half a century!'

'Doesn't invalidate a contract,' said Nigel.

Howard knew he mustn't be drawn into a quagmire of legal to-ing and fro-ing about which he and probably Nigel Hudson knew little. Making a show of shuffling papers on his desk, he said: 'Let's see where we are on this, Mr Hudson. What you've said is a big surprise, I grant you ...'

'... And a big story?'

'Potentially yes. I'm not a lawyer, but where the witness to a verbal contract is dead it suggests to me that the enforceability of the contract must be in doubt.' Howard was deeply sceptical about the credibility of the man's claim.

Nigel shook his head and simply said: 'Do you want the story or don't you?'

'We do, of course,' Howard replied. 'I'm not talking down the story; just want to make sure we have the facts straight. You've consulted a lawyer recently, I take it?'

Nigel confirmed that he had consulted a lawyer in the Virgin Islands and was seeing a lawyer here in town that afternoon. It was left that he would phone Howard the next day. The *Messenger* meanwhile would make some inquiries of its own.

'You're doing a lot of writing these days, Howie,' Cynthia remarked that evening when he told her about his day. She said it with affection. 'Rediscovering your roots?'

He felt a surge of affection for this woman to whom he'd been married for nearly half a century. He didn't know where it came from. 'Second journalistic childhood,' he replied, nuzzling her neck. 'But it's good to be back at the rockface.'

'Get away, Howie! Second journalistic childhood doesn't mean second teenager.' But she was laughing.

Howard's pleasure didn't last beyond the next morning. As a minor perquisite that Corporate HQ had yet to spot and stop, the chairman had the national dailies delivered to his home. He was leafing through the *Daily Mail* when his eyes fell on the headline

## BARONET AND HEIR LOCKED
## IN BATTLE OVER ESTATE

It was a big spread with a charming picture of Grawton Hall and extensive quotes from Roger and Nigel. The *Mail* had skilfully avoided the issue of whether Nigel's supposed verbal contract was valid. They had merely quoted claim and counter-claim, but they had moved quickly.

Howard was aghast. The newspaper had nothing more than he had or could have got. This was on top of the debacle when the *Sun* scooped him with the story of Benjamin and his transgender lover. He felt quite unable to face Rob Willis, the editor. He went into his study, closed the door and emerged half an hour later.

'You're late leaving this morning, Howie,' Cynthia remarked.

He knew he would struggle to pull this one off. He placed his hands lightly on her shoulders and looked her full in the eyes. 'I have a surprise for us, Cyn. We're going on a trip.'

'A trip? Where?'

'To Paris.'

'Paris? When?'

'Now. I've just arranged the tickets.'

'Now? Why?'

'Cyn, you're sounding like an echo. You like Paris, and at our age we should do spur-of-the-moment things.'

'Don't be silly, Howard. I've got the reading circle this morning, then I'm lunching with Marian and the girls. I can't just drop everything. Something's going on, I know it.'

He talked her round eventually. The truth was that Cynthia loved Paris. He phoned Marcia at the office to say he was called away on urgent family business, switched off his mobile phone and summoned a taxi for the Leeds Bradford Airport.

'I just know there's something going on,' Cynthia repeated as they rode to the airport.

'I'll tell you everything, but not right now,' Howard replied, gesturing towards the driver.

'Tell me you're not in trouble with the law,' Cynthia said in the airport terminal. 'Say to me that we aren't running away.'

'I'm not in trouble with the law. We can't talk about it in public. Just be patient please, Cyn, until we can talk in private.'

That moment came when they sat down for dinner. He took her to the fanciest place he could think of, which was Fouquet's in the Champs Elysees. They sat in a typically French enclosure bordering the pavement watching the endless streams of pedestrians and vehicles pouring up and down the boulevard. From the crisp napkins to the gleaming glassware everything promised a fine if expensive meal.

'Surely this is better than lunch with Marian and the girls,' said Howard.

Cynthia wasn't to be diverted so easily. 'Now at last you can tell me why we're here,' she demanded.

He told her how he had managed to get the *Messenger* scooped on its own patch not once but twice. He had bungled one of the most important and 'sexy' local stories – the contested future of the Grawton estate. He had left the story to be expanded the next day, allowing the *Mail* to slip through and publish first. He had promised not to reveal the existence of Benjamin's transgender lover, only to see the *Sun* break this cracking human interest story.

'I don't put pen to paper for years, and when I do I foul up not one major story but two,' he said. 'I just can't face Rob Willis at the moment. After the Benjamin business he told me off in public like a junior reporter. I must lie low until the fuss dies down.'

'Oh Howie, is that all? Is it really that important?' she responded.

'It is to me. It's so utterly shaming.'

Cynthia took Howard's hand across the table to cover an interruption while the waiter poured the wine. 'I don't think you did anything wrong,' she said after the man left.

'Oh I did. I admit it. I decided to keep Benjamin's secret. I ought to have known it would come out sooner or later, so I should have brought it out then and there. I sat on the Grawton story overnight so we could check the legal side of things, allowing the *Mail* to get in first.'

'You were just being conscientious.'

"I was soft, soft, soft. I put Benjamin the person ahead of Benjamin the news story, to be milked for every last drop of human interest. I waited with the Grawton story until it was too late. Maybe I don't know how the game is played these days. The devil of it is there was nothing wrong with the *Sun* and *Mail* stories. I know it and Willis knows it. They always said journalism is a young person's game. It's true more than ever in today's speeded-up world.'

His introspection wasn't done: 'I reported Roger Hudson's plan to sell Grawton quick enough. The truth is I thought the cousin's claim is tosh. I judged the story instead of simply reporting it. Elementary mistake.

'I must have lost my hunger to break news, if I ever had it. Maybe my time has gone, quite frankly.' Howard was being self-pitying and he knew it.

'So we're running away from Willis?' said Cynthia.

'Only for a few days.'

'Isn't that cowardly?'

'Yes, I'm a coward,' said Howard.

It was time to return to their hotel. It was raining; no weather for a stroll along the classically handsome avenues and through the homely side streets of the capital. Howard made to find a taxi, but Cynthia wanted to take the Metro.

'I love the Paris Metro, she said. 'The destinations sound so exotic: St- Germaine-en-Laye, Chessy-Marne La Vallee, Orry-la-Ville-Coye ...'

'... Aeroport Charles de Gaulle,' Howard added. Cynthia laughed, and hooked her hand around his arm. It was a rare moment of togetherness. As for so many others, Paris brought back the people they once were.

Emerging to the surface, they were confronted with a poster hoarding advertising '"Swinging London" Retrospectif'. Meg Denby's very familiar face stared back at them. It was no surprise. Paris had been the scene of one of her greatest successes when French critics had, rightly or wrongly, hailed her low-budget weepie as an ironic take on bourgeois society, a worthy successor to the icons of their own Nouvelle Vague movement. This was the film being shown now –*Le secret d'un veuf*.

'"The Widower's Secret"? I don't know that one,' Cynthia said with studied nonchalance.

'It's the French title for *As Far as the Eye Can See*,' Howard replied with equally careful casualness.

'Do you want to see it, Howie?' Cynthia asked nonchalantly.

'I don't think so, Cyn. I've seen it already.' Howard responded casually.

They walked on. Cynthia had never overcome the idea that Howard had married her on the rebound from Meg.

## PART TWO: MEG
## FIVE

WHEN Benjamin was thirteen it was finally decided that he must go to school. His education by Julia, the governess turned tutor, and the Reverend Hubert Atkinson, the retired vicar of Lowmere, was no longer seen as enough. These two had done a good and conscientious job within the limits of their knowledge and backgrounds. From Julia Ben had fluent Italian and no French; from Mr Atkinson he became accomplished at Latin and would have taken up Greek if Lord Chilcott hadn't vetoed the plan. The sciences were a closed book to Ben.

From time to time the grown-ups of the family – Meg his mother, his grandparents Lord and Lady Chilcott, even his uncles, Jeremy and Thomas – worried about the boy's solitariness, but all had their preoccupations and little was done. He mixed mainly with the adults, relieved by occasional visits from his cousins all of whom were younger. He was, however, allowed into the village each week to play football with the boys there.

Eton was the inevitable scholastic destination for Ben. Meg, on one of her visits to Lowmere, broke the news. It caused a fearful row. Ben, who had taken his temperament from the Italian Julia, turned his fury on his mother. 'I don't want to go away to school. I'm going to school here. You can't make me,' he stormed.

'Darling, you'll love it at Eton. You'll make lots of

friends and learn lots of new things,' Meg replied.

'Like what?'

She tried to think of subjects that were beyond the reach of Julia and Mr Atkinson. 'Chemistry and physics, for example. They have marvellously equipped laboratories where you can experiment with ...' Offhand she couldn't think of any experiments '... bunsen burners and things like that.'

'I'm not interested in that stuff,' said Ben. 'I like history and art and music. Mr Atkinson teaches me about those.'

Meg had a brainwave. 'They'll have computers. Everyone wants to know about computers these days.'

'What do computers do?'

'They allow you to write things quicker and make corrections without typing it out again and store things in the machine – like a filing cabinet without paper. You can play battle games on them. It's exciting!'

'Pah, that doesn't sound like any big deal.'

'And don't forget sport. They have all sorts of sport at Eton ... whatever you want really.'

'I do plenty of sport. I go riding. I play football in the village. Tennis with Uncle Jeremy and Sir Roger Hudson.'

Ben's initial fury had turned into petulance. Meg, whose anger was rising steadily, resisted telling him to do it 'because I say so', as one might to a young child. 'Darling, you must allow the grown-ups to know what's in your best interests,' she said.

This unwise sally reignited the boy's fury. 'No they don't,' he raged. 'I'm not going to rotten Eton, and you can't make me.'

'Ben ...'

Somehow he read her thought. 'If you're going to say

you can because you're my mother, no you're not – not really. How can you be my mother when you're never here? Julia's my real mother.'

That hurt. 'You know I'd love to be here with you all the time. It's because of my work,' said Meg.

'Madre di Dio! Who cares about your rotten work?'

Julia's future was another flashpoint. 'Of course she'll leave Lowmere once you're at Eton,' said Meg. 'I expect she'll go home to Italy. You can visit her, often.'

'She can't go home to Italy,' Ben shouted. 'Lowmere is her home. She's been here forever. I don't want to visit her in Italy. I want her to keep living here.'

'Benjamin darling, I know you want what's best for Julia. She wouldn't like it here after you've gone. She'd be lonely. She'd have nothing to do.'

'She can look after Montmorency.' This was Ben's cat, the second of that name.

'Sweetheart, that's hardly a full-time job.' And so it went on. The exchange ended with Ben rushing angrily from the room.

Meg was wrung out. She had played similar emotionally overwrought scenes several times in her films. The experience was nothing like the real thing. She retreated to the drawing room, swallowed two glasses of red from the decanter and phoned her friend Lucy Plessey.

'Stunts, you sound boozed' was Lucy's opening remark. Stunts was Meg's nickname in reference to the physicality of her action sequences, many of which she performed herself.

'Eeky, it was dreadful,' said Meg, using her private name for Lucy. No one beyond the two of them had discovered its origin. 'Ben just doesn't want to go. He shouted and shrieked at me. He said Julia was his real mother!'

'Poor you. He didn't mean it. He was upset.'

'Oh Eeky, what are we going to do?'

Lucy could always be counted on to be practical. 'He can't not go if you want him to,' she said briskly. 'Besides, it will do him good. He needs to be with boys of his own age.'

'He could run away from school, then we might never see him again,' Meg wailed.

'Come off it, Stunts. You're talking like a film script. That's not going to happen.'

The conversation left Meg feeling reassured. The effect didn't last long. She began to ask herself where she had gone wrong as a mother. Everything had seemed fine while Ben was growing up at Lowmere so she had no trouble in putting him out of her mind. Now at this critical crossroads she saw a procession of occasions where she had failed him. Above all, when had she demonstrated love; when had she hugged him?

It wasn't too late to change. She crept along the corridor to Ben's room, to tell him how sorry she was. Through the door she heard two voices – Ben's and Julia's. They were speaking in Italian, as usual, but she guessed what they were talking about.

Discouraged, she returned downstairs. She swallowed another glass of red en route for the gazebo, where she rolled a joint. It was impossible to smoke anything except tobacco in the house. Her parents were indulgent of alcohol, but strongly against drugs. The cannabis comforted her somewhat. Anything stronger would have to wait until she got home to London. She would leave the next morning.

In the end of course, Benjamin went to Eton. He learnt many new things, most of which his family would have disapproved of had they known.

Meg's drinking and smoking were a worry to Lucy. She often remonstrated with her friend.

'It's boredom,' Meg would reply. 'It's all very well for you, Eeky. You have your bookshop and a daily routine. I don't. What am I supposed to do when I'm not filming?'

'You have your work supporting the miners' strike,' Lucy pointed out. This was 1984 and the miners were in a bitter industrial dispute with Margaret Thatcher's government over pit closures. Television from around the world often seized on Meg as the most glamorous supporter of the miners.

'Yes, and it helps,' said Meg, 'but I've still got time on my hands. The old crowd and the old places don't have much appeal anymore.'

Certainly, her smoking and drinking were at their worst when she was between pictures. She haunted bars, sometimes alone, sometimes with some of the louche crowd who were her friends, so dressed down and with her lifestyle written all over her that she usually wasn't recognised. Not infrequently she ended the evening with a man – invariably younger – whom she hadn't known at the start.

Meg possessed a protean ability to transform herself when filming was about to begin. The frazzled appearance vanished; even the excess weight fell away. Although the scorching looks of the young girl had gone, she was revealed Cinderella-like at almost forty as a still beautiful woman. She was likely to remain so at eighty. Once the cameras rolled the toyboys were nowhere to be seen. Then she touched nothing more than occasional cannabis and some glasses of wine.

Meg's film career had got back on track after her rejection by Hollywood and the consequences for work in Britain. She was no longer the huge star. She had to watch as her former protégée, Alison Adams, took the roles that might have been hers. But she steadily increased her haul of solid and successful pictures.

Her comeback started with *The Importance of Being Ernest*. She was offered the relatively minor part of Cecily – a role she had played successfully on the stage long ago – and she grabbed it. She shed her years effortlessly. This was Meg at her best: the sparky naturalness, the drop-dead beauty. Having shown she could not only handle the part but also avoid inflammatory political appearances, Meg began to attract more jobs.

Her political work she continued under the radar. As the Seventies rolled on, Vietnam ended and women's liberation continued apace. This caused friction with her parents.

'That's why you can't find a husband,' Lord Chilcott said in exasperation. 'Who wants to marry a harridan?'

She responded warmly: 'A, I don't want a husband but I could find one if I did, and B, are you calling me a harridan?'

'I'm saying you often act like one!'

Now there was the miners' strike for Meg to support. In changed times the film producers, perhaps mindful of the adage that the only bad publicity is no publicity, didn't worry overmuch about their talent being involved with politics.

With no film in prospect, Meg was able to give her whole attention to the striking miners. Yorkshire was one of the main centres of support for the strike, and the seat of power of its leader, Arthur Scargill. She decided to base herself at Lowmere. She liked these men and felt for the situation in which they found themselves. Since the public knew her name, she would use that knowledge to help the pit-men. Having grown up in Yorkshire, she could understand their otherwise impenetrable accents. Underneath the roughness of speech and manner they had a genuine concern for each other and deep respect for women.

'These are my friends,' she told herself. She fancied she knew the miners as D.H. Lawrence (another of Haverstock's favourite authors) had done.

Breakfast at Lowmere was a running buffet. Not uncommonly each family member ate it alone. On this occasion Lord Chilcott entered the dining room to find Meg already in place.

'What are you doing today, darling?' he asked.

'I'm going to Orgreave near Rotherham,' she replied.

'I should have known better than to ask. There are no prizes for guessing what that is.'

'No, there aren't,' she agreed.

'Meg, do you see any contradiction between living in a place like this, and all the privileges it brings, and going to colliery gates and shouting abuse at the bosses?'

'No I don't. Justice is justice.'

Lord Chilcott picked up his *Messenger* wearily. 'I'm your father, but I admit defeat. I don't know why we're even talking about it. We've been having exchanges like this since you were twenty. I can't do anymore. Oh and by the way, Roger phoned last night. He'd like to see you while you're here.'

'Dear Roger ... I'm so busy, and what would be the point? When he phones again, please make an excuse for me.'

Meg set out for the Orgreave coking plant in a borrowed Mini, the family runabout car. The Aston Martin V8 stayed in the garage. She knew better than to display such luxury at what was effectively a hunger protest.

She reached the plant to find the biggest mass picket she had ever known. Both the miners and the police were numbered in their thousands. The pickets were penned into a field north of the plant, with police on three sides and a railway line making the fourth side.

She knew that the huge number of police meant only one thing – that they'd had advance information. It wasn't a comfortable thought that in the miners' ranks an informer was hidden. Even as Meg took in the scene, a large number of mounted police, truncheons flailing, galloped into the crowd. She learnt later that this was the third charge of the morning, and up to fifty horses were at the scene as well as almost sixty dogs.

In the face of the mounted charge the pickets scattered in pandemonium. Police in full riot gear followed up their advantage. Short shields and batons pushed and struck at the miners' front line to force it back. Strikers retaliated by throwing stones. These mainly bounced off the shields, but here and there an officer went down injured. Pickets fell too as the two sides locked together in hand-to-hand fighting.

'I wouldn't go any nearer, miss,' said a striker, who was clutching his arm, stunned and clearly injured. 'This is no place for a woman.'

Meg looked around. It was true. She could see no female police officers and very few female pickets.

Having scattered the miners, the police now re-formed their original line. This merely caused the pickets to move forward again, hurling stones and shouting insults. The noise of the battlefield, punctuated by the barking of the police dogs, rose to a new high. A fleet of lorries was leaving the coking plant. These were laden with the fuel supplies that the strikers wanted to stop. To jeers, the police escorted the lorries off the scene.

The infuriated pickets made yet another assault on the police line. With equal fury the hard-pressed officers pushed them back once more. And then the steam seemed to go out of the crowd. The police line had repeatedly held while the strikers' injuries were mounting. Many drifted away in the direction of the village.

An overwrought Meg was horrified at the violence and the savagery on both sides that she had seen. She knew this was to be a big setpiece event for the miners' cause. She had come to give moral support, but she had expected nothing like this. She saw injured men, some walking around nursing their injuries as best they could; others being treated by fellow pickets. Several police were seated on the ground with their injuries being tended. It emerged that even more police than pickets were injured that day – seventy-two to fifty-one.

'What can I do, what can I do?' Meg realised that she was talking to herself out loud. 'I must find Arthur and ask him how I can help.' The miners' leader could be seen in the distance near the police line.

As she made her way through the now thinning crowd of miners, she came across a man with blood flowing from a head wound. He was trying unsuccessfully to stop the flow with a small piece of cloth, which was stained red.

'Look, that cloth isn't enough,' she told him. 'This will help.' She took off her scarf and wrapped it across the wound, tying it tightly under his chin. 'But you need to get to hospital quick. I'll take you in my car.'

A man whom she hadn't noticed – probably a National Union of Mineworkers steward – stepped forward. 'We'll look after him. Thanks for your help though.' The injured man was hustled away.

The steward looked closely at Meg. 'What are you doing here, miss?' Then he recognised her. 'You're Meg Denby, aren't you? The lads are all very grateful for your help. You must come and talk to Arthur.'

Scargill could be seen walking up and down in front of the police line in a show of defiance. The police looked on expressionlessly.

Before they could reach him violence flared up again. Many of the now reduced number of pickets started to throw stones. The police were making ready to charge.

'The bastards!' said the steward. 'They wait until we're heavily outnumbered, and then they attack.'

They attacked with especial ferocity, driving their way to the railway line. The pickets fled for safety. Many reached a bridge. Others had to scramble down the embankment and across the rails. When the police reached the bridge they found themselves bombarded with missiles. Pieces of metal had been plundered from a nearby scrapyard. Meg, who had crossed the field behind the police, saw Arthur Scargill fall to the ground injured.

The police now acted to kill the protest. They formed a new line at the bridge while twenty or so mounted police rode in to disperse the crowd. Meg's last sight of the protesters was as they fled in ones and two and threes into the village. Here organised resistance gradually ceased. By mid-afternoon what became known as the Battle of Orgreave was over.

Meg came across a woman she knew well: Lesley Boulton of Women Against Pit Closures. Boulton was far from downcast. In fact, she was jubilant. 'We've got a photo,' she said. 'It shows a mounted policeman trying to hit me with his baton. That'll fix the bastards! They even attacked us in the village when we were sitting around doing nothing. A lot of the men had taken their T-shirts off and stuffed them in their back pockets. It certainly wasn't the sort of thing you'd do if you were planning to attack a seriously armed police force. You don't confront police like that in nothing but a pair of jeans and trainers.'

Meg knew where she had to go next – to a television studio to tell the world what she'd seen. She gave live interviews that evening to the two main British channels, BBC and ITV. She also recorded soundbites for French, German and American TV. All were delighted to have a well known personality as an eye-witness to the dramatic events of the day.

After some preliminary confusion among the foreign networks over addressing her as 'Lady Meg' – the Americans in particular struggled to understand why the daughter of a lord wasn't a lady – the interviews went well, she thought. The ITV interview was the most challenging:

INTERVIEWER: Meg Denby, you were at Orgreave today. Tell us what you saw.

MD: I saw scenes of incredible brutality and violence – police on horseback hitting stikers on the head with their truncheons; hand-to-hand fights when the police lashed out with riot sticks. Men bleeding ...

INTERVIEWER: Surely ...

MD: One man who I helped was bleeding so much that he nearly died, I'm sure.

INTERVIEWER: Surely the pickets engaged in violence too?

MD: They were defending themselves. It started as a peaceful protest and they were provoked.

INTERVIEWER: Do you consider throwing stones as 'defending themselves'?

MD: What do you expect them to do? The police repeatedly charged the miners' lines. They couldn't fight truncheons and riot sticks with their bare hands.

INTERVIEWER: I'm sure we'll all agree that violence during industrial actions is regrettable however it's caused. Miss Denby, what do you say to the idea that the police were there to keep the gates of the plant open for legitimate business?

MD: You mean the lorries taking out the coke to the power stations. I say that isn't legitimate business. They should stop until this dispute is over. The miners are only trying to stop unreasonable pit closures and save their livelihoods – and keep their wives and children from being on the breadline.

INTERVIEWER: The National Coal Board argues that closing uneconomic pits is reasonable as well as necessary.

MD: They would, wouldn't they? This country actually needs all the coal we can produce. Pits are only so-called uneconomic because of imported coal. I don't see why we should subsidise the jobs of miners abroad at the cost of our own people.

INTERVIEWER: There were around ten thousand pickets at Orgreave. That's a massive number for a 'factory gate' picket. They were bussed in from all over the country, and it's been claimed that many weren't miners.

MD: You're saying that's wrong, but there were an equal number of police and *they* were bussed in from all over the country. I don't know if everyone there was a miner. If they were a supporter, not a miner, what's wrong with that?

INTERVIEWER: We'll have to leave the question of flying pickets to another day. Now, Arthur Scargill, the miners' leader, has been injured and arrested. Did you see any of that, Miss Denby?

MD: Yes. I was near the railway line that the strikers fled over after the police charged yet again. I had a clear view of Arthur in a crowd of people. I saw him go down.

INTERVIEWER: It's disputed how he was injured – whether he was hit or tripped. What can you tell us?

MD: I wasn't near enough to be certain, but I'm afraid I think the trip idea is a little too convenient. The police were chasing individual miners and picking them off one by one, so why not the man they hate most?

INTERVIEWER: To be clear though: you didn't see the police hit Arthur Scargill?

MD: Not actually but ...

INTERVIEWER: Miss Denby, I'm afraid time is running out. On a lighter note, what do you say to the Barnsley miners, who have voted you the girl they'd most like to have a drink with?

MD: Yes please! I'm flattered. Tell me the pub and I'll be there.

Meg was still fired up when she returned to Lowmere late that evening. From the small drawing room, her father spotted her as she crossed the hall. 'Egalité Orléans!' he called out. Thanks to Haverstock's tuition the allusion wasn't lost on her. Lord Chilcott sounded more amused than irritated, unlike that morning's testy exchange on the same subject.

'I'm sorry, daddy,' she replied, 'I'm too tired to talk. I'm going to bed.' But sleep was out of the question. She phoned her friend Lucy from the extension in her room.

'Stunts, you were on fire! You wiped the floor with the ITV interviewer,' Lucy said.

'Well, good. He annoyed me. He was very biased.'

'You never let it show, which was great.'

'We've got them, Eeky!' Meg exulted. 'There's a picture, a close-up, of a mounted policeman hitting a woman with a baton. The police will have to pay for that. And fifty strikers were injured. They'll want compensation too. It'll be a turning point, I tell you.'

It proved to be no turning point. The strike was to

drag on for many months. The picture never had the impact Meg hoped. Controversially, most newspapers ignored it. South Yorkshire Police later paid £525,000 in compensation and costs to thirty-nine pickets.

# SIX

MEG was stoned when the news reached her that Everard Hughes had died of Aids in Hollywood. As she sunk into a dream-state, she found that they were making love on the terrace at Lowmere. Of the many places where they had coupled the terrace wasn't one. They were surrounded by curious bystanders, cheering them on.

Then she was lying in the huge bed at Everard's magnificent home high above Los Angeles, with its picture window giving an uninterrupted view of the Pacific Ocean. She was soaking even before he pulled off her panties and pushed her to the ground. He entered her immediately, deep and hard. Everard was ever the swordsman. She climaxed quickly, and a few seconds later so did he. 'God, I'm tired,' he announced and promptly fell asleep. The Lowmere bystanders, who had somehow appeared at the scene, applauded.

And then it was Lucy, shaking her into the present and helping her down from her drug high. She felt nothing about Everard's death. She was sure this wasn't suppressed desire or denial of grief. She hadn't loved him for years. If anything, she hated him for what he did to her and their child.

Everard's death rated just a few lines in the newspapers. His star had fallen far and fast. Two consecutive turkeys and the revelation that he was living openly with a man, thus destroying his appeal to his core support group, young women, had left him out of work for years. All that remained was the round of US chat shows and shopping mall openings. Meg learnt the news from the paper, and it was a safe bet that Ben had heard too. He was probably being bullied even now about his gay father. Rather than phone him and risk another strained conversation, Meg decided to visit him. It was harder to answer in monosyllables when you're face to face.

As she pointed the Aston V8 to the west for the short run to Slough and then Eton, Meg reflected that she had done the right thing by forcing Ben into the school. To say he had settled in well would be an exaggeration, but he was clearly coping. Yet his surly half-greeting reminded her that he still blamed her for putting him there.

'How's everything with you, darling?' she asked. 'All right.' 'What have you been doing lately?' 'Not much.'

Rather than pursue this uphill exchange, she decided to get quickly to the reason she was there. 'Benjamin, I suppose you've heard about your father.' 'I have.'

'I'm so sorry you had to hear about it from the newspapers. That's how I heard. I didn't phone because I knew you'd have heard already.' 'It's all right.'

'Actually, I'm so sorry that you've lost your father. It's rotten for you.'

'Actually, it isn't. I never knew him or ever heard from him. He treated me very badly.'

'I know, darling,' said Meg, 'but he was still your father. He treated me badly too, but I couldn't help feeling a bit sad when he died.'

'I've had a rotten time with the other boys,' Ben confided. 'They say I'm the son of a poofter, bum bandit, faggot ...' 'I get the point, Ben.'

'And they say things about you, too.' 'I don't want to

know!' said Meg hastily.

'Was he very gay?' Ben inquired.

'I'm not sure there are degrees of gayness,' she replied. 'Some people can be both gay and straight. Obviously Everard wasn't one hundred per cent gay.' This was a strange conversation to be having with her son about his father and her lover. She added quickly before Ben could say anything: 'He made his choice and stuck to it. A lot of it was because of this one man he met – Jason.'

More to herself than to Ben, she went on: 'Everard said he was disappointed with women.' What he actually said was that women were too easy to turn on. They were like light switches. Liberated woman as she thought of herself, she couldn't use such a crudely sexual image to her son. 'It's sad for any man to feel like that.'

Ben said nothing. He seemed to have lost interest in the subject. 'Can we have tea somewhere?' he asked.

They found a teashop in Eton High Street, where under the influence of meringues and scones with lashings of jam Ben opened up a bit about his life at school. As she returned to London Meg told herself that things between them had got a bit better. She knew, however, that he had not once used any direct address – he hadn't called her 'Mother' or any of its equivalents.

At home boredom beckoned, as she often complained to Lucy. Meg examined herself in the full-length bathroom mirror one evening, and didn't like what she saw. Her face was puffy and the eyes tired; lines were starting to appear. Her shoulder-length hair was lank, but at least no grey hairs were to be seen. Around the midriff was unmistakable flab. At least the breasts were okay, she conceded, and thighs, legs and bum showed no detectable cellulite. It was too depressing for the stuff of a million men's dreams. In response, Meg put her hair up in a librarian's bun, slipped on a pair of black-rimmed glasses, donned a worn fishermen's sweater and made for the Potting Shed.

This was a night club that she had used for years. It was well beyond its prime. The decor was at least full-blooded – guests sat on fertiliser bags, the tables were upturned seed boxes and the table lamps were housed in flower pots – but what had once seemed quirky now seemed simply naff. As long as the money kept coming in the management saw no reason to change. The aristo-theatrical crowd, Meg's set, had long ago moved on, to be replaced with the new money of Thatcher's Britain – the stock market traders, the property developers and the like. She continued to use the club because she could be herself. The regulars who knew her left her alone; most of the other guests never recognised her. The manager, remembering the old days when celebrities were ten a penny, never pointed her out to visitors.

Meg made her way to the bar and ordered a double gin and Italian. The barman was absolutely gorgeous. He was tall, lean and straw-haired with the guileless look of a farm-boy – and the accent of a street-wise South Londoner. The boy's T-shirt and jeans (topped with a gardener's apron) clung to an obviously toned body. He couldn't have been more than twenty.

'I don't believe I've seen you here before,' Meg said.

'I started yesterday.'

'How's it going?'

'I like it, although it's hard to keep up with all the different drinks and the large rounds people order.'

'You're doing a pretty good job, I'd say.' The boy

smiled. 'Will you have another gin and It or will you wait for your friend?'

'I'm not expecting anybody,' she answered. 'I'm having a little private celebration – a promotion.'

'Congratulations! Let me guess. You're something important in an office. A bank maybe?'

'Not even warm! I'm Maggie and I'm a librarian.'

'Nice to meet you, Maggie. I don't read books, I'm afraid. I look at my dad's *Sun* newspaper sometimes.'

Meg could easily understand it. She hadn't got him down as the bookish type. That wasn't his appeal. After several gin and Its Meg felt at peace. Around midnight the boy left the bar, then reappeared in his street clothes. He explained that his shift was over.

'Come round to the other side of the bar and have a drink,' Meg invited.

'I'm afraid it's against the club rules, Maggie. I'd like to, of course.'

'Then let's find a drink somewhere else,' she said. The boy agreed with this. Outside the club Meg suggested that the obvious place was her flat, to which he further agreed.

'This is a beautiful place you have here,' he remarked.

'I wish it were mine,' Meg said. 'I'm looking after it for a friend.'

They both knew what was going to happen, but the boy had his sense of priorities. 'I'm starving,' he announced.

'Poor you,' said Meg. 'I don't suppose you ate all night. There's not much here. Bread and cheese if that will do.'

He wolfed it down, at the same time talking in his South London accent and spraying salivated crumbs over the table and floor. He's so delightfully natural, thought Meg. He's like an animal. Animals don't worry about table manners. They only worry about getting at their food.

'Have you got any weed, Maggie?' he asked.

She rolled a couple of big joints. They clung together on the sofa smoking them. Reality disappeared bit by bit, and they fell asleep.

Meg awoke late that morning with the sun streaming through the bedroom window. She was lying naked on top of the bed covers. She had no idea how she got there. Beside her the boy, also naked, was asleep. His hairless chest rose gently up and down.

As he lay on his back, she could see that his body was perfection. Beautifully proportioned, not an ounce of surplus fat, with all the incipient vigour of youth. His flaccid member looked so cute nestling in its thicket of hair. It was neither too big nor too small, too thick nor too thin. Once again the idea of an animal struck her. He was a beautiful animal that would act out its urges without forethoughts, afterthoughts, second thoughts, doubts, worries.

The boy was evidently dreaming. He mumbled words that Meg couldn't make out. Then his member slowly rose up until it was proud and erect and about three times its former length. She found herself instantly aroused. 'Very well, let's turn dreams into reality,' she told herself.

Gently so as not to wake him, she mounted and impaled herself on him. She worked herself up and down, enjoying the hardness of his entire body. She found time to wonder what difference she was making to his dream. Still asleep, he responded to her rhythm with his own pushes. They rolled together on to their sides where, with a little gasp, he came. Meg was short of her climax and was left feeling out of sorts.

He woke up while he was still inside her although limp. 'Oh, hello,' he said in the way one might greet someone met unexpectedly in the street. 'Hello, you,' she answered, drawing lines with her finger around his perfect face and neck.

Meg didn't remain out of sorts for long. Fully awake now, the boy explored all over her body, the public parts like the neck, arms, shoulders and legs as well as the private parts. His roving hands had nothing of the gentle about them. Rather, they urgently needed to know everything there was to know about this woman. Meg was more than ready when he entered her with a determined thrust. He made a few more pushes and quickly came. But Meg had come before him so was well satisfied.

After this there was nothing for the boy, and he soon left. Would he ever find out that he'd fucked Meg Denby, film star, she wondered. What a notch on his bedpost that would be! When he'd gone she realised she didn't know his name.

Meg felt a deep sadness after the episode of the beautiful barman. Another mechanical, meaningless coupling. Even so, she wanted more of him. He was irresistible, so gloriously a child of nature. She returned to the Potting Shed the next night to find him.

'You mean Darren?' said the manager. 'I'm sorry, Miss Denby, he's left us already. Said he couldn't take the evening work. They're all the same, these boys. They want the money, but they don't want to do the work.'

'If you'll let me have his forwarding address I'll write to him.' Meg didn't trouble to invent some respectable reason for contacting Darren. The manager knew her so well it would have been pointless. In any case, she didn't care and neither did he.

'We don't have an address for him. We paid him in cash, and he left with everything up to date.'

So that was that. At least Meg knew there would be another one along soon – a thought she didn't dare articulate to herself.

She wondered where was the man who would love her for herself, who would sometimes simply be content with a cuddle? Who of the many men in her life had really loved her? Arnold Haverstock, her first real lover, had done so, she was sure, but she had been a child and he was well into his thirties. Their relationship drifted into that of an uncle and a favourite niece, and then a father and a daughter; now they exchanged Christmas cards, nodded when they saw each other at social events and Haverstock – who she realised was an ageing roué – was settled with another Meg-type. Howard Jenkins could never forget he was making love to a film star and a viscount's daughter. Roger Hudson had shown his love through his constancy. She had grown up with him as the boy from the manor next door, and it would have been like fucking your brother. As for Everard, had it been a deception – a beard for his gayness, as he once claimed – from the start?

In this mood Meg drank and smoked even more heavily than usual. She filled up with snacks when she ate at all. The pounds piled on. From the gates of a colliery, having motored there from Lowmere, she gave a disastrous TV interview on behalf of the striking miners. She waved a placard in the interviewer's face, fumbled her words and seemed to be tipsy, although whether from drink or tiredness was uncertain.

'Oh Stunts, if you go on like this the miners won't want you,' said Lucy.

'I didn't sleep well at all last night,' said a chastened Meg. 'I was worrying about how the miners' children will eat if this strike goes on and on.'

'The television viewers didn't know that. They just saw somebody who looked and sounded drunk,' Lucy riposted in her usual down-to-earth way.

'I know,' said Meg.

# SEVEN

AT last a new film materialised. Meg was to play a widow with a teenage daughter. Her character meets and in due course marries a handsome bachelor (co-star yet to be chosen), whereupon the daughter and the step-father fall out. Meg loves them both, but may have to choose. The working title was *Tug of Love*.

Within a few days Meg looked and sounded like another person. Her eyes grew brighter, her voice sounded happier and her skin was clearer. Even the excess weight had fallen off.

'I just don't know how you do it!' said Lucy. 'I only have to look at a piece of cake and I gain a pound.'

'Simple,' Meg replied. 'I don't eat cake when I'm doing a film.'

The male lead in *Tug of Love* was announced as Bob Curzon. Meg was delighted. They had appeared together years before in *As Far as the Eye Can See*. They were lovers for one night only, falling off the chastity wagon on the last day of the shoot at Great Torrington. It was a magical interlude for them both. They returned to their partners, and hadn't seen each other since.

When the phone rang in the flat one evening, Meg in her new persona was entirely sober.

'Is this still Meg Denby's number?' a male voice inquired.

Meg, disguising her voice, admitted it was. One had to be so careful about stalkers, intrusive fans and general nutters.

'Thank heavens for that,' said the man. 'This is Bob ... Bob Curzon. It is you, isn't it, Meg? The studio people made a song and dance about giving me your number even though we're to work together. I was worried that you'd moved and changed your number.'

'Yes it's me, Bob. Same old pad and same old number,' she replied lightly.

They agreed it was marvellous to be working together, and that much water had flowed under the bridge. 'Let's meet for lunch,' said Bob. 'Just us. So much to catch up with.'

'Will your wife (Meg couldn't remember her name) be all right with that?'

'I'm not with Meryl anymore.'

'I'm sorry.'

'Yes well, I'll tell you about it when we meet.'

She noticed that he didn't ask whether she was with someone ... someone after Everard. He knew about Everard. The whole world knew about her and Everard, or at least the whole of Britain, much of the rest of the English-speaking world and France (where *As Far as the Eye Can See* had been a totally unexpected hit). They were to meet at a bistro in Charlotte Street, which was near Meg's Bloomsbury flat.

Bob rose from the table as she entered the restaurant. He was dressed very simply in designer jeans and a light blue shirt. She hadn't seen him with glasses before. With his black-framed spectacles he looked more like a with-it professor than an actor. At around six feet he was filmically a perfect match for her five-feet-eight. Meg wore loose-cut slacks and an angora wool jumper in green, with a silk band over her long black hair.

'You look gorgeous as always, Meg,' Bob said.

'Thanks but I've almost reached the age when "gorgeous" sounds either ironical or charitable,' she returned laughingly.

'"Almost" perhaps but certainly not yet!'

This comfortable exchange set the tone for a long, lingering lunch that they both enjoyed.

'I'm sorry Hollywood didn't work out,' Bob said. 'Shut me up if the subject's too painful.'

'It was painful at the time. Not anymore.'

'They didn't deserve you – look at it that way. They're putting that Alison Adams in all the big stuff. She's not a patch on you as an actress. She can register only one emotion, and that's neutral!'

'Oh Bob,' Meg laughed, laying her hand on his arm. 'Do you mean I can register two?'

'You know I don't mean that!'

Then it was Meg's turn. 'I'm sorry about you and Meryl,' she lied.

'Don't be. It was years ago. She's a senior professor now. As she climbed the academic ladder I think it worried her that she was with a mere actor. Not a proper job – that sort of thing. Feminist she may be, but she's "Professor *Curzon*". She's kept my name – God knows why.'

'And there have been people since?'

'Hundreds. I have to fight them off all the time. And you?'

'The same. So many to fight off I'm thinking of putting sandbags around my house!'

They parted without having mentioned their one night of love. They didn't need to. Meg was comfortable with the memory, and she sensed that Bob was too. She didn't invite him back to the flat. This one was better developing gradually.

It was no ardent wooing. Meg, determined not to be hurt twice by Bob's rejection, made no move, and if she was waiting for his phone call, it never came. Once filming began, however, they fell easily into each other's company. Between takes they sat and laughed together. They started leaving work together until word got back that the production crew were enjoying ribald humour at their expense, taking them to be an item already.

"We're both single so where's the harm, but let's not gratify their dirty little minds!' Bob joked.

From then on they left the studio separately.

Outside of filming they spent a lot of time with each other. They enjoyed quiet dinners, raucous parties and long walks along the banks of the Thames, where Meg under her disguise of drab headscarf, baggy jumper and thick librarian glasses was never recognised. She was surprised that Bob appeared to want nothing more than friendship. This after all was the man who had seduced her at Torrington. Perhaps he was still scarred from his break with Meryl; perhaps, although Meg hated to admit it to herself, he didn't want to add himself to the long list of her failed relationships. Typically at the end of an evening they locked together with their tongues urgently exploring the depths of each other's mouths. She felt again the strangeness of tasting someone else's saliva. Then Bob would break away and disappear into the night.

Eventually all dropped into place. One evening their kissing had been especially fervent. As they embraced Meg pulled Bob's shirt away from his trousers and made her fingers do a little dance around his chest. In response, he slipped his hand down her blouse and underneath her bra to caress the erect nipples. When their mouths parted for air Bob murmured: 'It's very symmetrical – one up and one down!' They both collapsed giggling.

'It's a long way home to Wimbledon,' he said. He had never complained about it before.

'You can stay at my place tonight,' she replied '... or forever.' Bob moved in that night and never again took the late train to Wimbledon.

'Why did it take us so long?' Meg asked the following morning as they lay comfortably in her large double bed. Both were naked.

'Well, why did it?' he said.

'It's rude to reply to a question with a question.'

'I'm known for my rudeness,' he responded and left it to her to start.

'I was waiting for you,' said Meg.

'That doesn't sound like the talk of a famous women's libber.'

'There are limits to women's lib!'

Bob raised himself up and lay across her. Their bodies stuck together as he kissed her lightly.

'I'm in love with you, Meg,' he said. 'I waited because I wanted to be sure that you have feelings for me. When you invited me to move in with you, I told myself you do. At least a little bit.'

'Oh I do,' she gasped. 'And not a little; lots.'

With that she took told of his member, which stiffened at her touch, and guided it into herself. He moaned and came very quickly. 'Now rub me off,' she said.

They could hardly keep their hands off each other in those early days, in private and in public. It turbocharged their love scenes in *Tug of Love*.

'Phew! Were you people acting?' Simon, the director, joked. By now they made no secret of being an item.

'It's disgraceful behaviour for two people pushing forty,' Meg said when they were back in the privacy of her dressing room.

Bob proved himself to be the same considerate lover as he was at Torrington. Mostly he waited until Meg was ready; he didn't satisfy himself until he knew she was satisfied. During her times of the month he was content to kiss and cuddle. At times, though, he wouldn't be gainsaid despite her reluctance. Then he would work patiently away, his hands finding one erogenous zone after another until, invariably, she melted.

He was also the first man since Arnold Haverstock who could match her in the intellectual interests that Haverstock had implanted in her. He could talk knowledgeably about music and painting and in particular literature. 'Although,' he admitted, 'thanks to Meryl my knowledge is a little skewed. For example, I know more about Anne Bronte than Jane Austen. Now Anne is an underrated writer, but I'd struggle to say she was greater than Jane Austen!'

Anne Bronte's *The Tenant of Wildfell Hall* was a favourite of Bob's feminist ex-wife. This tale of a woman who leaves her abusive husband to set up her own household – scarcely thinkable in its day – chimed with Meryl's liberationist views.

'I can't believe it,' Bob said one day. 'Here am I and here are you.'

'That's undoubtedly true.'

'I mean, what have I done to deserve you?

"You deserve me because you're Bob!'

'You're a big star and I'm a jobbing actor. You're the

daughter of a lord and I'm just middle class.'

'Hey, hey ... what's that got to do with anything?'

'Like calls to like,' said Bob.

'Not always it doesn't,' she replied, hugging him. 'Lords and ladies are just people like any other. We'll go to Lowmere and you'll see.'

Bob soon recovered from his crisis of confidence. He was in high spirits when they reached Lowmere after an easy run up the M1 and A1 (M).

The abbey was bathed in evening light as they stood on the terrace each with a glass of wine. Not a sound was to be heard except the cawing of rooks.

'I'd no idea it was so beautiful,' said Bob. 'How can you bear to be away from such a fabulous place?'

'It's being away that makes it fabulous, or at least makes one appreciate how fabulous it is.'

'Very wise, my lady!'

Bob had never ridden a horse. Meg, whose memory didn't reach back to when she first sat in the saddle, taught him. He was an apt pupil. After only a few sessions he could mount the horse in style and, with a good approximation of control, get it to trot and canter. 'We'll leave galloping for next time,' said Meg.

As it happened, the local foxhounds were meeting that day at Lowmere. Meg's much loved brother Jeremy had come from London for the occasion.

'You know I don't hunt, Jer,' she told him. 'It's cruel.'

'Put a sock in it, Meg! You grew up with horses and hunting. And besides, the exercise will do you good,' Jeremy implored.

It was true that she badly felt like a gallop across the fields. Nor was it much fun riding on your own. Memories of bracing rides across a sunny, snowbound landscape, followed by a hot bath and tea and scones with lashings of jam, rose before her. Somehow she allowed herself to be persuaded.

Bob easily agreed that he wasn't ready to go with them. 'In any case, I wouldn't want to. I don't agree with fox-hunting,' he said. 'I'm surprised you do, Meg.'

She felt herself blushing. 'I don't actually. It's just for once – to keep Jeremy company. We probably shan't find a fox, and if we do it will probably get away.' It sounded pathetically weak even to her.

Bob said nothing more and soon put the issue out of his mind. He didn't feel strongly about it. The occasion was to have worse results, however.

The hunt came to a gate admitting on to a lane. The riders had to wait to get through. Here they encountered a group of protesters. To her horror, Meg recognised some women's lib friends including the leader, Suze. It was clear that they had recognised her.

The horse was standing still waiting its turn at the gate. Meg and the women stared at each other in a mixture of surprise and mutual embarrassment. Suze eventually broke the silence: 'Meg, I wouldn't have thought it of you.' Her tone was more sad than angry.

'It's just this once,' Meg replied, for the second time that morning with blood suffusing her cheeks. 'My brother Jeremy is down from London and ...' She tailed off. 'The fox doesn't know that,' someone shouted. 'Blood will out,' called another.

Mercifully for Meg, her turn at the gate came and, with a mumbled 'Sorry', she rode away.

The incident had taken less than five minutes but everyone knew it would have consequences.

Bob was the first man after Everard that Meg had

brought to Lowmere. He passed the Chilcott test. 'I like your new friend, darling,' said Lady Chilcott when Meg found herself alone with her parents. Bob was still in the separate bedroom that he was decorously occupying.

'He's more than a friend, mummy,' Meg replied.

'Well, your fiancé if you prefer.'

'It's about time you had one of those,' put in Lord Chilcott.

'Oh daddy!'

'Actually, Bob seems a steady sort of chap,' her father continued. 'Much the best of the ones we've seen up here. Hard to believe he's an actor.'

'Is that supposed to be a compliment, daddy? Next you'll say he's so good he could be a politician.' This was a reference to Lord Chilcott's former ministerial career.

'Touché!' said her father.

Bob reciprocated the Chilcotts' approval.

'I like your parents,' he told her. 'They seem very straightforward, down-to-earth people.'

'What did you expect? People dressed in coronets and robes, spending all day bossing the serfs around?'

'No, but it must change you having all this.'

'Must it?'

'Perhaps it does more than you realise.'

Bob expressed a wish to meet Benjamin. 'I want to learn everything about your life,' he told Meg. She agreed reluctantly, not knowing what reception they would receive. They found the boy in the art studio at Eton, painting in water colour.

Oh hello,' he said. They might have been acquaintances chanced upon in the street. Meg took him in her arms and tried to kiss him. Bob noticed that Ben, already half a head taller than his mother, tipped his chin upwards so she was pointing her lips at his Adam's apple. She admitted defeat.

'Ben, this is my friend Bob.'

'Are you living with my mother?'

Meg made to stop him, but Bob just smiled. 'I suppose I am, Ben,' he answered honestly. 'Is that very bad?'

Ben thought for a moment. 'It's all right,' he allowed. 'Are you an actor?'

'Guilty, your honour! I'm in the film your mum is making right now. I play the hero. Unfortunately, the hero and the heroine's daughter don't get on, and the heroine – that's your mum – has to choose. That's why the film is called *Tug of Love*.'

Bob's open, natural manner was winning Ben round. 'What do you think of my painting?' the boy asked. 'It's Windsor Castle seen from the Great Park. I'm working from this sketch – see? – that I did when I visited.'

'I think the painting is excellent and very clever. I love the way you've put people in to add foreground interest.'

'They're from my imagination. The scene would be static otherwise.'

'Static indeed!' said Bob. 'That's what my paintings were like when I tried to be an artist. I could only do matchstick figures, and I couldn't do trees to save my life.'

'Trees are difficult,' Ben agreed.

Later, in a moment when he was alone with Meg, he said: 'I like Bob. He's an OK guy.'

'You've made a hit with Ben,' Meg told Bob as they drove back to London in the Aston. 'In fact, you're picking off my family one by one!'

'That's the idea,' he replied, putting an arm affectionately round her waist. She sensed that he wanted to ask her why her relations with Ben were so strained, but wisely he said nothing.

The wrap party for *Tug of Love* (the working title having survived as the final title) was soon upon them. It had been a happy shoot, helped by the entire cast and crew's forbearance of the super-brat who played the daughter, fourteen-year-old Juliette Smiles.

'I don't need to act that I dislike Juliette!' was how Bob summed it up.

Rarely was the name Smiles – her real one – so wide of the mark. When she wasn't acting, Juliette spent most of her time sulking. The dressing room was too hot, too cold. The coffee was likewise too hot, too cold. The taxi that took her back and forth was late. The person playing opposite her was talking too fast, too slow. Why couldn't she have flowers in her dressing room? They'd given her those in her last picture. Why couldn't she change the line (as it was written it didn't suit how she saw the character)? Sometimes she suggested to the director that the shot would be more effective from another angle. Simon just ignored her.

None of this was apparent as Juliette rose to make a little speech (by invitation). In a winning, perfect-daughter manner, she said: 'Meg, thank you for being a lovely mum! Bob, in the film we don't get on, but really you're the loveliest person. That goes to for Simon, our director, who's helmed this picture that will be a huge hit. It's been the happiest film I've worked on. (For Juliette, a star from the age of four, every film she worked on was 'the happiest'.) Meg and Bob, I'd just love you to be my real-life mum and step-dad – although I suppose the ones I have already might say something about it!'

Everyone laughed, the sulks and the tantrums apparently forgotten.

Later that night, sated with wine and sex, Meg declared: 'I've never been happier.'

'Let's get married,' Bob replied.

'Mmm, yes please.'

'Consider it done, milady! Right after I get my divorce from Meryl.'

# EIGHT

AS summer turned to autumn and autumn to winter, it became the best of times for Meg. She was happy with Bob, at home with him in the flat and in their highly visible social life. She was once again part of a golden couple. It was like being on the town with Everard again. The newspapers, used to Meg's serial relationships as gossip column fodder, fell eagerly on this turn of events. She even managed to smile about a *Daily Mail* story:

### MEG THE 'WALLFLOWER' GETS HER MAN

Beauteous actress Meg Denby has put her wild child days behind her, it seems. The 39-year-old has traded her hectic social life with a succession of dates, many of them younger than her, for domestic bliss with actor Bob Curzon, 40, her co-star in the forthcoming picture *Tug of Love*.

No more need Miss Denby be a wallflower in her lonely North London flat, where the pair are nestling happily. Friends say they look increasingly like a fixture.

'Happiness comes from being with the one you love, not from chasing here, there and everywhere,' says Miss Denby, improbably. It must be the real thing this time.

> In her twenties Meg Denby was considered the most beautiful of her generation of actresses, but she has never married. She had long relationships with author Arnold Haverstock and the late bisexual actor Everard Hughes. She has a son, Benjamin, 15, by Hughes.
>
> Miss Denby, who is the daughter of a viscount, failed in her shot at Hollywood after moguls objected to her affair with Hughes and her support for radical causes. She has since rebuilt her career in Britain, although she is currently a vocal supporter of the striking miners.
>
> Rising star Bob Curzon was married, but it is not known whether he has been divorced. He lived up to his quiet man image by telling us: 'Meg and I are in love. There's nothing more either of us wants to say.'

Meg was as happy as she'd ever been. Background sadnesses, like Ben's continuing coldness and the miners' strike dragging on towards what looked like inevitable failure, disappeared in Bob's quiet, reassuring presence. She drank and smoked less.

Bob refused to follow her in her use of cannabis and cocaine. 'I've tried them and I liked them too much. That's why they're dangerous,' he explained.

'Everything in moderation!' she replied.

'There's nothing moderate about you, Megs,' he said softly, ruffling her hair. 'Seriously though, you ought to stop. Especially the coke.'

'Tomorrow – maybe. It's the boredom, Bob. What are we supposed to do between pictures?'

One way was to take up the long abandoned pastime of painting. Bob returned to the flat one afternoon to find Meg hard at work at a water colour.

'Why are the people's faces green?' he asked.

'What?!'

'Oh, didn't I tell you I'm colour blind?'

'Beast!'

He found a stash of her paintings in a cupboard. They had been done years before during her time with Haverstock. Bob put them on the walls around the flat. 'Soon we'll be able to charge admission to the gallery,' he joked.

The sex continued to be sensational. Bob's self-control was amazing. It drove Meg wild when he placed himself directly outside her safe harbour, touching the harbour walls in fact, and waited before he sailed in. Meg had never felt more fulfilled as a woman. One night she pointed to the packet of pills beside the bedside table.

'I just need to forget to take those, and ...'

'Not yet, darling,' Bob said. 'The time isn't right. Soon.'

Meg continued her support for the miners' strike. Often she stayed at Lowmere, within easy reach of many pits. The snag was this meant frequent separations from Bob. After the bustle and action of the days, the loneliness of the nights hit her hard. As the alcohol, a supposed nightcap, kicked in at last, she became desperate to hear Bob's voice. She phoned him at the flat.

'You didn't see me on TV this evening then?' she asked.

'I was out.'

'Oh ...?'

'Squiring the latest starlet to blow in from America

around town.'

'Beast! If I believed you I'd be worried.'

'But despite the pulchritudinous charms of the aforesaid, who may or may not be imaginary – and especially her boobs – I'm missing you desperately.'

'I'm missing you too.'

'I'm missing you more.'

'I'm missing you most.'

It was time to return to London.

In the new year Bob went away for three months to make a film in South America. For Meg, however, no picture was in sight. The destructive pattern resumed. The painting stopped, the drinking and smoking increased. She started haunting the late-night bars and clubs again, often alone.

'Welcome back, Miss Denby,' said the manager of the Potting Shed. She wasn't drunk, and saw enough to wonder whether the manager felt sad for her. Her younger brother Thomas sensed some of what was going on, and passed a sanitised version to their parents. They pressed her to make more frequent visits to Lowmere, staying away from the miners.

It was now nine months since the Battle of Orgreave. The National Coal Board, backed by Margaret Thatcher's government, had stayed firm over pit closures and maintaining supplies to power stations, and it was clearly winning. Meg continued to stand on picket lines and give media interviews for the miners, but she sensed the strike could end only one way.

Support for the strike had never been total with a dispute over the legality with which it was called. Over the long weeks some of the strikers drifted back to the pits. 'Hunger scabs' appeared. These were strike breakers, many of whom had been pickets, who returned to work to feed their families. Eventually, the union's strike pay ran out. The trickle of returners threatened to become a flood. The National Union of Mineworkers executive committee had to act.

Meg took a phone call from Kevin, the Yorkshire official through whom she co-ordinated her activities on behalf of the miners. She was alone in the flat, collapsed on her bed and lost in a haze of alcohol and grass. It took many rings before she realised it was the telephone, and that the best plan was to answer it.

'You'll hear soon enough – just switch on your radio – but I wanted to tell you first,' said Kevin. 'The national executive have voted for a return to work. The strike is over.' His voice was breaking up.

'Oh, I don't understand.'

'There's nothing not to understand, lass,' he replied. 'The union's run out of money, the men must feed their families, the strike's over.'

'That is terrible,' she said after a delay. She was taking a long time to articulate anything.

'Tell me what to do,' she said. 'I can give one of my TV interviews. I'll phone them.'

After a long pause of his own, he replied: 'I think we're covered for the moment, lass. Mebbe later. I'll be in touch.'

Meg was aware enough to know that now even the miners didn't want her.

It soon became clear that the strike, lasting days short of a year, had achieved nothing beyond a delay in the closure of the pits at the centre of the dispute. Worse, from the union point of view it had given the government the springboard for a root-and-branch reform of trade union law. This was duly carried out in the years to come.

Meg saw things more personally. 'Those poor men,' she said. 'They've suffered for a year for nothing. They'll lose their jobs. Their families will be hungry. I can't bear to think about it.'

She apologised to Kevin for being drunk on the day the strike ended. She didn't mention the cannabis. 'I totally see why I couldn't do the TV interview. It won't happen again,' she said.

She heard his hesitation. 'Oh, but it already has, Meg,' he said.

'What do you mean?'

'That time on *Panorama* ... And the one from the colliery gates ...'

Then she remembered. She had fumbled her words, asked for questions to be repeated and gone off on long digressions. She thought no one had noticed.

'It's not a problem anymore, Kevin, honestly. There were special reasons. And anyway, if it's recorded that would be safe.'

'Lass,' he replied. 'You've made your contribution. We all have. The strike's over.'

Except it wasn't quite. In some areas the strike lingered for two weeks more. The Kent miners were the most militant, organising pickets around the country. Arthur Scargill, the miner's president, was stopped by Kent pickets when, accompanied by a Scottish piper, he marched the miners of Barrow Colliery in Yorkshire back to work. Scargill said, 'I never cross a picket line,' and marched the men away from the colliery.

Meg had heard that at Bulcliffe Wood Colliery near Wakefield miners' wives were to hand the men carnations as they returned to work. The flowers symbolised heroism. The pit was an easy run from Lowmere. Once again leaving the Aston discreetly in the garage and borrowing Lady Chilcott's mini, she headed off to join the wives. None appeared to recognise her and, if they thought she was an improbably glamorous miner's wife, no one said anything.

Meg handed out her flowers as the men filed past, mumbling 'Thanks, lass' or 'Thanks, love'. They were a sad, downcast bunch, their brio long gone. The most powerful union in the country had been beaten, and the men knew it.

She spotted a TV crew filming the event. She walked over to them. 'Can I help at all? With a comment or something?' she asked.

The young reporter jumped as if he'd seen a ghost. After all the drably dressed working women he was confronted with this apparition of style – dressed down but still looking chic, and very beautiful.

'Yes, I think so. Thanks,' he answered enthusiastically. Then he recognised her. She admitted she was Meg Denby. 'Just a moment please.' He was on the phone. She couldn't hear what he was saying. He came back to her and told her: 'Studio says the segment is already full up with material. So thanks but no thanks.'

It had never happened before. Journalists queued to get her quotes and soundbites. Meg thought back to her last conversation with Kevin. The miners must have spread the word that she no longer spoke for them, and couldn't be relied upon, so now even the news media didn't want her.

Lucy Plessey knew how deep Meg's depression was, but she felt powerless to do anything about it.

'Don't keep telling me I look terrible,' Meg complained to her friend. 'Do you think I don't know it?'

'Stunts, I really thought you'd put all this behind you,' Lucy said. 'Now you're settled with a man who loves you – who will be back home with you in a few days ...'

'And I'm no longer a wallflower,' Meg interjected with a flash of her former good humour.

'Yes, the *Mail* got that right! And Bob's only away for three months. You're still beautiful, your career's back on track, you have a loving family ...'

'Shut up, Eeky! Don't lecture me like a marriage guidance counsellor.'

'I'm only showing you how lucky you are. You don't need the booze and the drugs and the – to be frank – gigolos. Now me, I have nobody; no Bob in my life, and I probably never will have.'

But Lucy's lecturing had no more effect than her alternative strategy of sympathetic listening. What turned the trick for Meg was the announcement of the premiere for *Tug of Love*. She had to look good for Bob, too. Once again, the hair grew more lustrous, the eyes brighter, the voice lighter, the face clearer and the body tauter as the excess weight fell away.

Lucy exclaimed: 'You do it every time ... I wish I knew how. I'd bottle it and sell it.' Privately, she knew that her friend was metamorphosed a tiny bit less each time. The signs were barely perceptible, but ultimately the lifestyle was not to be beaten.

Meg was looking forward to the premiere. The idea of it was spoilt only by the inevitable presence of that frightful child so-called star, Juliette Smiles. Darn it, thought Meg, the girl would be too young to see the film in a cinema. Why should she be allowed to watch it at the premiere? Meg thought about tipping the police off anonymously that an under-age person was attending the event. Tempting. If she timed it right, the police would rush round with sirens blazing and extract Juliette just as she was walking up the red carpet.

It was a dream. Juliette at the premiere was as obnoxious as ever, on the red carpet and off it. She was to enter the cinema first, ahead of the two principals. Playing up to her tomboy persona, she wore not a ball gown but a clearly expensive pair of slacks with a plain, ruched blouse. Jewellery dripping round her neck and from her arms contrasted ill-advisedly with the otherwise simple attire.

Accompanied by her mother, Juliette progressed slowly up the red carpet, turning, smiling, to left and right, milking the applause from the onlookers. Meanwhile, Meg and Bob sat waiting in a limousine out of sight of the cinema entrance.

'Could she go a bit slower, do you think?' Bob grouched.

Without warning, Juliette performed a cartwheel, and a second one, to the delight of the onlookers. The mother looked on approvingly. The pair then disappeared into the auditorium to thunderous applause.

'What was that?' asked Bob. They could hear but not see what happened.

'We don't want to know,' Meg replied. 'It'll only put us off. Come on, our turn.'

The director, Simon, had been ecstatic that Meg and Bob would walk the red carpet arm in arm. 'Lovers in the picture and lovers in real life. They'll go bananas for that!' he exulted.

Certainly the response of the crowd was enthusiastic as they entered the cinema, every inch a golden couple of filmdom. Juliette and her antics were quickly forgotten, it seemed. Bob was elegant in black tie while Meg wore a ball gown in cerise, her long black hair strikingly offset with copper jewellery at her neck and on her arms.

They sat next to Simon, who was in high spirits as the title sequence rolled for *Tug of Love*. 'They're going to eat this up!' he predicted. It didn't seem that way to Meg as the film proceeded. The audience reaction was muted. Laugh lines produced no more than titters; action sequences generated few gasps. Juliette played herself, making it easy for Bob to convince as the wicked step-father since he couldn't stand her for real. Meg, on the other hand, struggled to present a woman racked by the need to decide between her daughter and her husband. She was on surer ground in a supermarket scene when she had to choose between broccoli and green beans. She could easily see that after two hours the audience simply wouldn't care what she decided – would have been happy if the domestic civil war carried on for years, so long as the film ended now.

'We can fix it,' Simon whispered as they filed out of the auditorium. The party after the show was full of the usual congratulations and declarations that the picture was wonderful. Across the room Meg saw Juliette holding court. She at least in her brattish self-centredness would have told herself that the film was a hit. The other chief figures in the production knew otherwise. So did the critics.

The reviews in next morning's papers were uniformly negative, some slightly less so than others. Most focused on the weakness of Meg's performance in the key role of the wife and mother. The *Guardian's* critic was especially savage:

> Meg Denby utterly fails to convince us that she is the mother of busty, bouncy teenager Samantha (Juliette Smiles) or that Sam's feud with her step-father (Bob Curzon) is more than a minor irritant. In fact, Miss Denby as usual in her recent roles remains intent on playing the ingénue herself.
>
> She was a delightful child-woman in *As Far as We Know*, but that was a decade and a half ago and the middle-aged matron can no longer pull it off. The lines are beginning to show.

When Meg read this she burst into tears.

'Don't take any notice of one stupid review,' said Bob.

'But it's not stupid, it's true,' she sobbed. 'It's all I can do, play silly girls. It's all I've ever been able to do! I'm thirty-nine years old.' Then with a flicker of spirit: 'Why the fuck am I still playing silly girls?'

Bob grabbed her by the shoulders. 'Now listen to me, Megs. You know that review's not true. You play the parts that producers and directors want of you. That's the business we're in. It's not your fault if you have to play younger. I know and you know that you can stretch yourself when the chance comes along.'

She was still crying. 'I should have stretched myself in this film, and I couldn't do it. The review is right. Oh Bob, the film will be a flop because of me. I've let you and Simon and everybody down.'

Meg was bereft. Nothing that Bob tried brought her out of her low mood. The film did as badly on distribution as everyone expected. Meg became afraid that she was finished in the film business. All this was on top of the debacle of the miners' strike.

She was referred to a nerve doctor in Harley Street.

'Perfectly sensible reaction to external events,' said the man cheerfully. 'The film for which you had high hopes has flopped, and you fear for your career. You were committed to helping the miners, and their strike failed. On top of that, you feel they no longer wanted you.'

'Exactly,' said Meg.

'I'll give you something. Don't worry. But before I do I want you to tell me the good things in your life.'

'Well, there's Bob, my fiancé. My son, Benjamin. My good friend Lucy, who I've known for years.'

'So there you are,' the doctor continued, 'lots of people loving you and supporting you. As for those worries, you're a famous person, Miss Denby; a star, in fact. Do you have any hard evidence that studios no longer want you?'

'No,' she admitted.

'So it's just a phantasm. Banish it! What's happening to the miners is sad, but you can't bear the woes of the world on your shoulders.'

'I know, but ...'

'No "buts" please! Our first duty is to ourselves, and your duty right now is to become your usual cheerful self again. Your son's at boarding school, isn't he? Easter is almost upon us. He'll be back for the holiday, no doubt. That must be something else to look forward to.'

Meg felt cheered up just from having had the doctor's brisk, no-nonsense analysis. And the pills in her pocket would help. Despite their difficulties she was looking forward to Ben being with her over Easter. Her son got on well with Bob. They would all have a good time.

'Let's not go to Lowmere. There's plenty of room here,' said Bob. 'I think a young man would prefer London.'

'The walls are very thin. All the sounds carry,' said

Meg.

'So?'

'In the bedroom ... You know. Children don't like to think about their parents having sex,' Meg pursued.

'We could always stop for the duration of Ben's visit.' Bob responded. Meg pulled a face. 'Better idea,' he added. 'We could fit it in when he goes out. "Quick, he's gone round the corner to buy Coca-Cola. He'll be back in five minutes."'

They fell together giggling. In the end they decided to go to Lowmere for Easter. Ben had other ideas. 'I want to go to Italy,' he announced.

'But, Ben, Easter's one of those times when families get together,' said Meg. 'Everyone will be at Lowmere. They are all so looking forward to seeing you again.'

'I don't care. I must go to Italy and see Zia Julia.'

Meg rashly rose to these remarks. 'There's no "must" about it, Benjamin. You "want" to go to Italy. It's not the same thing. And Julia's not your "zia".'

It was Ben's turn to rise. 'She's more of an aunt to me than you've ever been a "madre"!'

The ensuing row was the ugliest they'd had. In the aftermath, the doctor's pills could make little headway with Meg's feelings. Because Ben didn't control any money of his own, or at least not enough to finance a trip to Padua, he was forced to spend Easter at Lowmere. He was surly throughout the visit, spending his time in his room or in solitary walks through the estate. He returned to London as soon as he could to see out the rest of the Eton holiday at the family's townhouse with his Uncle Thomas.

Meg's mood continued low after she returned to London with Bob. The effect of the happy pills was destroyed by flashbacks of her row with Ben. Nor could she tell herself it was a one-off event: it was of a piece with their relationship overall. The doctor declined to double her dose. She turned once again to alcohol and drugs, losing herself for days at a time in a haze of unknowing.

Lucy was aghast. 'This is so dangerous, Stunts,' she said. 'Mixing your medicine with alcohol and cocaine could be lethal. Please, please stop.'

Meg felt ill, but didn't want to stop.

Bob looked on in despair. The funny, intelligent, beautiful woman he loved had gone. One day he told her that a part had come up for him in a film shooting in Spain, and he would be gone for two weeks.

She understood enough to challenge him. 'You never said anything about a film,' she complained. 'We share everything, don't we?'

'Indeed we do, darling. This was very last minute. It's just a cameo part. I'll be back before you know it. Lucy will keep an eye on you.'

'I don't need anybody to keep an eye on me.'

'Yes you do, Megs. I mean practical things like shopping while you don't feel like going out. You've not been well – very understandable with all the blows you've had lately.'

Meg was not to know there was no film in Spain; he just had to get away.

When Bob returned a fortnight later he found that Meg, with her protean capacity for reinvention, was back to her usual self. She told him: 'I've stopped the grass and the coke and pretty much the booze – just some wine now and again. And, do you know what, darling? There'll be a film for me soon.'

Bob, on the other hand, looked dreadful. He was red-eyed and gaunt, and had developed a stoop.

'What on earth's the matter?' she asked.

'Nothing much,' he replied. 'I'll tell you soon.'

That night in bed he turned away from her. It had never happened before. She drifted resentfully into sleep. When she woke up she reached out to him, but he was up already, pottering in the kitchen. 'Come back to bed,' she called.

He refused. He insisted that she dress because he had important news to give. With gathering apprehension she came to him. She saw that he struggled to look her in the eye. That she was back to her ravishing best added to Bob's anguish.

'Megs darling, my love, I'll love you till I die, but I simply can't go on like this.' She couldn't take in what he had said. 'Your ups and downs ... the drink and drugs – they're destroying us both.'

She still didn't understand the full import of what he was saying. 'I know I've been through a bad patch. It's all behind me now.'

'Darling, it isn't. Not for good. We can't make a go of it.'

She began to see where he was going. 'We can talk about it; we must talk about it,' she pleaded.'

'Sorry, darling, I've thought and thought about this for months. There's nothing more I can say,' he replied.

With an intuitive leap she saw what had happened in the past two weeks. 'There was no film in Spain,' she accused. 'You've been with Meryl.' He admitted it. He had turned to her in his desperation. They had rediscovered each other and he was returning to her.

Meg could hold it in no longer. 'It's not true! It's not true!' she shrieked. 'You and I are going to be together forever!' Her body shook with great spasms of grief.

Bob forced himself to hold her to him. 'Darling, I'll always love you, but it's not meant to be. Don't make it worse for both of us.' He would have preferred her to be angry. Instead, she slumped prostrate across the kitchen table. 'I can't leave you like this, Megs. I'll send Lucy to you.'

He slipped out of the flat for the last time. Meg still lay on the table, barely conscious. Eventually she slept.

When she awoke she took a few seconds to remember what had happened. Then she felt complete and utter desolation. The world was drained of meaning. The ceiling seemed to be falling in on her. Now Lucy was at her side with a bowl of soup.

'Drink it. You'll feel better,' she commanded, practical as ever.

The neurologist diagnosed a total nervous breakdown, and commanded rest and quietness. 'Keep the newspapers away from Miss Denby,' the doctor said. 'They'll only upset her.' Meg spent the time mainly looking at the video cassettes that Lucy provided (having pretended that the television was broken) and thinking. Wherever she started from, her thoughts always came back to the same four traumas: the failure of her film and her rejection by those who mattered most: the suffering miners, her son and the man she loved. She couldn't get past these spectres.

At night she woke, rigid with shock from flashbacks. It was always the same moment in the same scene. She was shrieking at Bob: 'It's not true! It's not true! You and I are going to be together forever!'

Somehow the news leaked out that she and Bob had parted. Meg didn't see the newspapers so she was spared a gossip item that picked up the familiar 'wallflower' theme:

## SAD MEG A WALLFLOWER AGAIN

Unlucky-in-love actress Meg Denby finds herself a wallflower again after fellow thespian Bob Curzon walked out.

Friends of the couple were shocked at the break-up.

'We thought this one was for keeps,' said one. She held out no prospect of a reunion because Curzon has returned to his wife, Meryl, a university lecturer.

Miss Denby, 40, seen as the most beautiful British actress of her generation, has had a string of failed relationships and has never married.

To add insult to injury, her latest picture, *Tug of Love*, is currently bombing at the box office.

'The bastards!' Lucy said to herself. 'Don't they know there's a real suffering human being behind every bit of cheap gossip published in a newspaper for entertainment?'

Meg was at last declared well enough to go to Lowmere. The rock in her life, the place of safety to which she had always returned and would always return. In this benign environment Meg steadily rallied. What she called her four spectres were always there, but the night-time flashbacks became rarer. She began to see her life with special clarity – how she had in fact failed with everything that mattered.

She had clearly failed to build a loving relationship with Benjamin. The boy disliked her, possibly hated her. Wasn't loving and giving priority to one's children supposed to be the most important thing in life? Yet she had farmed out Ben's care so she could enjoy her fame and her life in London.

She so enjoyed being a film star, yet was she really an actress? The reviewer was right: for twenty years she'd played the same part, which was herself, or an idealised version of herself. It had become absurd ... the forty-year-old ingénue. When faced with a real part, the mother in *Tug of Love*, she'd been found wanting.

She had failed in her relationships with men. The loves of her life – Arnold Haverstock, Everard Hughes and now Bob Curzon – had all for their different reasons left her. Even that boring provincial journalist, Howard Jenkins, whom she agreed to marry when she was pregnant with a child that wasn't his, had abandoned her. She had persistently turned Roger Hudson away when he was perhaps the one man who wouldn't have failed her.

She had campaigned against the American war in Vietnam and for women's liberation and in support of the miners. Vietnam had been a success. She was proud of her part in it. But it was a long time ago. The other causes seemed to get along perfectly well without her. None of the women or the miners' representatives had contacted her in the weeks when she'd been ill. She knew why. The miners could not be expected to forgive her for appearing on TV drunk. That shaming incident when the hunt protesters found her out with the hounds meant the women no longer saw her as one of them. Can it be true, she asked herself, that she couldn't rise above her aristocratic background, that 'blood will out' – the insult hurled at her by one of the protesters?

Meg told herself she wasn't depressed, but all in all she couldn't think of much that she'd done right with her life. It didn't matter too much. A sort of acceptance settled on her.

Lucy, visiting for the weekend, was delighted at how she found her friend and former patient. 'You're looking so well, Stunts. I can hardly believe it,' she said.

'Oh Eeky, I feel well at last,' Meg replied. 'On Monday I'll phone Harold to see what's around for me.' Harold was her agent. 'Time to get cracking again.'

'That's great, Stunts – but only if the doctor agrees. You don't want to go back too soon.'

'Of course.' Meg gazed through the open French windows, across the terrace to the park in its late summer fullness. 'You know, Eeky, it's very beautiful, isn't it? Everything became tangled in London. I've had so much time up here simply to think about things. I see it all clearly now.'

Lucy rose from her chair spontaneously, and without another word embraced her friend.

That clarity of vision, once achieved, never left Meg. Everything fell into place. One day, during a brilliant September when the first hints of autumn were showing, Meg took the Aston and headed east to the coast. Her destination was Flamborough Head. She parked the car, found a piece of paper in her bag and wrote a note. It read:

*My dearest parents*

*I'm so sorry. I love you all. You, Benjamin, Jeremy and Thomas, Lucy. I've failed at everything. I'm so tired. I can't go on. This is the best way.*

*Sorry. All my love*

*Meg*

She looked at the cliff edge a hundred yards away. She ran towards it, then stopped as she saw over the edge to the rocks far below. Jagged, hostile rocks. I can't do it, she told herself, I haven't got the guts!

Close by, a young couple with their children knew very well what she meant to do. 'Stop! Don't ... don't do it!' the man cried. He began to move towards her. 'Don't panic her!' the woman shrieked, but the man kept moving.

That decided it. Meg started to run again. He was within five yards of her, ready to rugby-tackle her to the ground, when she threw herself over the edge. As she fell Meg had enough time to know she'd done the right thing.

# PART THREE: JUSTICE

# NINE

IT was a fine September day in 2013 – the twenty-eighth anniversary of Meg Denby's death. Howard Jenkins took himself to Flamborough Head. He didn't tell Cynthia, his wife, where he was going. He sat on the grass and gazed out to sea. Somewhere near here it had happened all those years ago. He didn't know exactly where; didn't want to know.

Howard had debated with himself whether he should bring a bouquet of flowers – come to think of it, he had never known Meg's favourite flowers – and throw it over the edge in remembrance. He rejected the gesture as mawkish. Instead, he simply sat there and let the memories of Meg come flooding back.

It was the first time since her death that he'd been to Flamborough Head. He'd felt compelled to come, although he knew that it made matters worse. Somewhere near here Meg's lifeless body had lain battered and broken on the rocks. He couldn't bear to think of the mutilation of that beautiful girl, the most gorgeous and radiant of her generation, who had laughingly greeted him on that first occasion and touched his arm in a gesture of spontaneous friendliness.

He had pursued her after that, ground her down really, until in the end she agreed to marry him. Then he was too scared to do so. He couldn't believe he was worthy of such a person. He had been an everyman among the beautiful people. That mind-blowing occasion at the Aux Plumes de Mes Tantes restaurant with Meg, Arnold Haverstock and the rest ... he had been almost tongue-tied. He supposed he must have resourcefulness and durability – 'a knighthood for sticking around,' as they said behind his back at the *Messenger* – but these were not qualities he'd ever desired.

He had run away from the wedding – that was the only way to put it – and married Cynthia instead. He had taken up with Cynthia again in the way one takes up a favourite old coat. Meg never married. She had numerous liaisons, many of them played out in the glare of media publicity. Loveless, pointless couplings probably. None lasted until finally it had come to – this. Was it really all because of him?

'Are you all right?' Two hikers, a boy and a girl, stood over him. 'You don't look very well.'

Howard snapped out of his reverie, and saw himself as they must see him – an old man sitting on his own and looking lost. He felt tired just looking at the two in their youthful vigour. The girl was about the same age as Meg when he had first met her. She was fetching – yes, that was the word – in her hiking shorts and walking boots. Femininity meets manly pursuits.

'I'm quite all right, thank you,' Howard replied. 'I was remembering someone I used to come up here with for walks. My wife. She died.'

The pair didn't seem entirely convinced. 'I'm so sorry,' said the boy. '... As long as you're OK ...'

Howard realised they probably thought he was about to throw himself over the cliff. In answer, he mumbled, 'I'd better get home now,' and walked determinedly away from the cliff edge. He glanced back several times, and saw that they continued to watch him from a distance.

The visit to Flamborough had made clear to Howard what he hadn't admitted to himself over all the years – that he was burdened with guilt over how he had treated Meg. Perhaps this was the secret of the sleepless nights he suffered. In these closing years of his life he felt an overwhelming need to be freed of the burden. He wanted absolution, but not the sort some find from priests and others from prayer. He wished he could be put on trial leading to a verdict of guilty. That would be a sort of punishment, after which he would be free. Since a trial wasn't an option, someone who was there at the time might help with an honest view. But who? They were mostly dead. Everard Hughes was dead. Arnold Haverstock, in whom Meg continued to confide after their split, was dead, as were Lord and Lady Chilcott. Meg's brothers, Jeremy and Thomas, were alive. They had only been on the edge of the story; nor were they the sort of people he could imagine opening his heart to in an intimate conversation. Lucy Plessey! Meg's closest friend, who knew the story in its entirety. She would be best of all to talk to. He hadn't seen or heard of her in almost half a century. He must find Lucy Plessey. But was she alive or dead?

He drew an immediate blank with a Google search. Howard knew that these days 'social media' appeared to reveal everything about everybody. He didn't use the wretched stuff. Now he wished he did.

He found Emily, the young reporter, in the staff restaurant ('canteen' in his younger days with the *Messenger*). 'If you wanted to find someone after fifty years, how would you go about it?' he asked her.

'I'd use hypnotic regression to tap into my past life,'

she joked. 'Seriously though, Howard, I'd start with Facebook.'

'Surely a person that old wouldn't have a Facebook site – account – whatever you call it.'

'Page. And you'd be surprised. Oldies are some of the most prolific users of Facebook, Sharing pictures of their grandchildren, and stuff like that.'

But there was no Lucy Plessey on Facebook. Perhaps she had no grandchildren, or was an oldie who was an exception to the Facebook rule. Or was simply dead.

'In that case,' Howard announced, 'I'll do it the old-fashioned way. I'll go to – their – last known address and pick up a trail. Who knows? Maybe they'll still be there.'

Once again Howard deceived Cynthia. A white lie, he called it, to avoid causing her distress. Inventing an urgent consultation with Corporate HQ, he set off for London. He had forgotten the name of the bookshop and the street. He was confident, however, that he could find the location.

The street was exactly as he remembered it. Of the bookshop, any bookshop, there was no sign. A wave of nostalgia flooded over him. He had visited this shop many times. Lucy had been his lifeline to the elusive Meg. The nostalgia was so severe that he had to sit on a bench to recover himself. Finally, he set about asking at the building where the bookshop had been. He was certain he had the right place. A well remembered blue plaque next door still commemorated an obscure eighteenth century scientist. In the place of Lucy's bookshop was a Costa coffee shop. Entering, he found that all the staff unpromisingly looked about twenty. The place was packed. When he reached the head of the queue, he ordered a small americano with hot milk on the side, and asked if he could have a quick word with the manager.

The young man identifying himself as such looked a shade older – all of twenty-two. 'I believe there was a bookshop before it became a Costa,' he said. 'We had a regular customer who used to talk about the old days in this street. But it wasn't an independent shop. It was a national thing ... Waterstone's? No ... Borders. Yes, that was it. Borders.'

'That's a pity,' said Howard. 'Borders has closed down in the UK.'

'A couple of streets away is a Waterstone's,' said the manager helpfully. 'Somebody there might know something.'

Indeed they did. The staff here were older. Howard addressed himself to a girl on the till who looked all of twenty-three. She'd never heard of Borders, but helpfully knew somebody who might. 'Hey Jack!' she called over to a man mainly concealed by a book stack. 'Gentleman asking about a shop called Borders round the corner. Didn't you used to work at a place like that?'

Jack turned out to be a man of about sixty, who confirmed that he'd worked at Borders. Howard explained he was trying to trace the owner of a previous bookshop in that building.

Jack looked at him quizzically, then seemed to decide that Howard was too respectable or too old to be a debt collector or a tax inspector. 'I can't help you much,' he said. 'It's all going back a good few years. Borders bought out an independent bookshop run by a lovely lady called Rosemary. Don't remember her name or what she called the shop.'

Howard felt a frisson of excitement. Surely that would

be Rosie, Lucy's daughter. 'Was it "Plessey" by any chance?' he asked.

'That's it! Rosemary Plessey. Lovely lady.'

'What happened to Miss Plessey?'

'About a year after she sold to Borders, we heard she'd died. A young woman too.'

'It's her mother I'm trying to reach. Can you think of anyone around here who might know something?'

Jack said that Miss Plessey had been friendly with a woman called Georgie, who as far as he knew still worked at the nearby Spar grocery shop.

Georgie remembered Rosemary Plessey well. 'And I knew the mother too – of course I did. Lucy. A very practical person. But nice with it. Rosie was more of a dreamer. Haven't seen Lucy since Rosie died. After she handed over the shop to Rosie, Lucy retired to some place in Devon.'

'Exeter? Plymouth? Torquay perhaps?'

'No, much smaller,' said Georgie. 'I remember Lucy saying it was such a small place that everyone knew your business before you knew it yourself! Began with ... let me see ... W. Yes that's it, W. Wa... Wi ... Wo ... Sorry ... I just can't remember.'

Howard thanked Georgie gratefully. He was soon to discover that around one hundred and eighty towns or villages in Devon begin with the letter W. At least it was a start in his search for Lucy Plessey.

'You're going to Devon?' Emily said with astonishment. 'It'll take you a month of Sundays to search the electoral registers.'

'I know,' Howard replied. 'It's a massive job but at least I'll be on the spot when I've found – them.'

'*If* you find them,' she pointed out. 'People can have

their names left off the register seen by the public.'

Howard knew it would probably be a lengthy search away from the home and office. It meant lying to Cynthia again. He told himself it was to spare her the pain of knowing that after almost half a century he was still working through his feelings for Meg Denby. He invented a residential course on the latest techniques for senior management. Trusting soul that she was, Cynthia would never check.

'Aren't you a bit old for management training?' she commented.

'Never too old to learn!' he replied lightly.

Deception was so easy really.

In Devon, Howard installed himself in a series of council offices and public libraries, with the tedious task of searching the electoral registers. He prayed that he wouldn't have to look at one hundred and eighty places. He started with market towns and large villages on the basis that 'it was such a small place that everyone knew your business before you knew it yourself' didn't have to mean a hamlet. Coming from London, Lucy would find most places in Devon small.

He was soon in luck. He checked the large village of Winkleigh, north of Dartmoor, and found the name – Lucy Plessey. Just that one person registered at the address. Howard wasn't certain that Lucy would want to see him. If he found out a phone number and called it, she might simply refuse to speak. If he door-stepped her (in the parlance of his former trade) he would have a chance to talk himself over the threshold.

There was a chance he'd call at an unsuitable time – that after almost half a century he'd walk in to find a drama in progress, with the washing machine springing a leak, the milk boiling over or a pot of paint spilled on the carpet. It was a chance he had to take.

Lucy's address was a neatly kept bungalow in a new part of the village. Geraniums and begonias continued to make a good show despite the lateness of the season. Feeling again the butterflies of a junior reporter facing a difficult cold contact, he rang the bell. He wasn't sure he would recognise Lucy. Meg would have been seventy now. Her friend must be about the same.

The door was answered by a very old and poorly dressed woman. She wore a shapeless jumper and a drab skirt; her wispy grey hair simply fell where it pleased. This couldn't be the owner of such a well presented property, but who was she?

'I'm sorry to bother you,' Howard began. 'I'm looking for Lucy Plessey.'

Without hesitation and with a confidence that her appearance belied, she answered, 'I am Lucy Plessey.' She was totally unrecognisable from the woman he remembered. She must be well over eighty. Then he remembered he had never known her age.

Lucy showed no sign of recognising him. 'Howard Jenkins,' he offered. 'I was in the area, and I thought that after so long I might drop in to say hello.'

It sounded ridiculous, but Lucy merely said 'yes'. From her silence on the point, he assumed she remembered him. She seemed to be neither glad nor sorry to see him. She gestured him into the house and asked if he'd like tea. While she was making the tea Howard sat and looked around the sitting room. Befitting her former work, the room had many shelves of books. There were several pictures of a striking youngish woman. That must be the grown-up Rosie. He spotted a picture of Meg and Lucy hugging happily.

'It's so good to see you after all these years,' he ventured.

'Yes.'

'You're looking well.'

'Thank you. How did you find me?' Lucy was still in neutral. It was very strange. He remembered long, jokey conversations with Lucy in her bookshop. In some ways the talk had been easier with Lucy than with Meg because he didn't have to try. He told her about Georgie in the Spar shop, and managed to suggest that Georgie had pointed him to Winkleigh. He didn't want to admit that he'd searched in a haystack and found the needle. Fortunately, she didn't press him.

'I heard about Rosie,' he said, turning his head to one of the pictures. 'I'm very sorry.'

'Thank you. Cancer.' She seemed not to want to say anymore. Ask an open question, the journalist in Howard reminded him.

'What brought you to Winkleigh? It must be a huge contrast after London.'

'That's why I came to Winkleigh. I picked on Devon, and I spotted this house.'

It was the longest utterance Lucy had made since he entered the house.

'What do you find to do in a village like this?'

'Oh, plenty.' It was back to brevity. Perhaps she sensed that after forty-five years he hadn't called for casual chat. He decided to come to the point.

'Lucy, I've wanted to talk to you about a certain matter. About Meg and me. You were there. You saw everything.' She was listening, cupping her chin in her hand like a don conducting a seminar.

'It's almost thirty years since Meg ... you know. I went to Flamborough Head ...'

'What did you expect to find there?' she interjected.

'Nothing, of course. But I felt I should, after everything. I thought about things I should have done years ago. Lucy, I want to ask you: do the family hate me?'

'No,' she answered, 'the family don't hate you. Why should they?'

'Because of what I did to Meg ... because I ran away from the wedding. Perhaps everything went downhill for her after that.'

She came to life at that. 'That's nonsense!' Howard remembered her direct manner of old. 'Meg had lots of good years to come. She didn't go downhill for years after you – left. That was for many reasons, but you weren't one.'

'Thank you, Lucy. I've been so unhappy.'

'You don't need to be. You and Meg weren't right for each other.'

'Then why did Meg agree to marry me?'

Lucy settled herself in the chair and thoughtfully reviewed the question before replying. Howard pictured her leading a study group for the University of the Third Age. He wondered where was the nearest branch, here in the back of beyond.

'It was the late Sixties,' she said. 'Despite the image we have of the Sixties, it was in many way still a time of traditional values. Meg underneath everything was a traditional person. She didn't like the idea of being an unmarried mother. The family hated the idea, too. The Denbys have four centuries of aristocratic breeding behind them, yet they can be strangely middle class in their values. Especially with their women. Everard was the father, but he wouldn't marry her. You would.'

'I thought the child was mine,' said Howard.

'There you are then. Meg let you think that, so you might say she was unfair to you, not you to her.'

'Did you know?' he pursued.

'Of course I knew. As you suggested, I knew everything, but it wasn't my place to tell. You could say that *I* was unfair to you. All in all, you have nothing to reproach yourself for, Howard.' It was the first time at this meeting that she'd used his name. 'You have many happy memories of Meg, as I do. We must cherish them.'

'I remember that dinner at Aux Plumes de Mes Tantes. It was the first time I met you. Everything started for Meg and me from there. I feel privileged to have known her.'

'We all feel privileged to have known her,' Lucy responded simply.

A thought still troubled Howard. 'Perhaps because of me Meg ended up an unmarried mother, which you said she and the family hated. Then why do you say the family don't hate me now?'

Lucy smiled for the first time since he entered the house. 'I suppose you could say their hatred was overtaken by events. The Sixties became the Seventies, and nobody cared about unmarried mothers anymore. What you did was for the best, believe me.'

'You don't know how glad I am to hear you say that.'

Lucy added: 'Meg was devastated when Arnold Haverstock and Everard Hughes left her; Bob Curzon even more so. You were ... well, irrelevant.'

For the first time in his life, Howard was delighted to feel irrelevant.

# TEN

IN the weeks that followed his meeting with Lucy, Howard felt a great weight removed from his back. She had given him the absolution he sought by showing him in her brisk, no nonsense way that he had been of little consequence in Meg's life; therefore anything he did, even publicly jilting her, must have been of little consequence.

Howard even set about his joyless work at the *Messenger* with new vigour, although spreadsheets of financial projections – invariably gloomy – weren't his forte. After the fiascos of his interviews with Ben and Nigel Hudson, he sometimes wondered what his forte was.

Cynthia noticed his cheerfulness. 'You're very chipper these days,' she said.

'I suppose it was the affirmation of the anniversary party,' he replied disingenuously. 'It showed me my fifty years with the paper haven't been in vain!'

'The expression is "My living has not been in vain". I've always known the *Messenger* is your life, Howie!' she responded, only half-jokingly.

He found himself wondering about Benjamin, whom he knew remained at Lowmere. Now that he, Howard, had come to terms with his past, it seemed yet more of a tragedy that Ben wasn't reconciled with his mother's memory. He gave Ben a call and reached him at the first attempt.

'I'm pleased to hear from you, Sir Howard ...,' Ben said, sounding it.

'"Howard" ...'

'...Howard. I wanted to phone you. Guido has arrived. I'm sure you're very busy, but if you can spare the time I'd like you to meet him.'

Once again Howard found himself motoring up the long drive to Lowmere. It was more than concern for Ben that brought him there; he was frankly curious to see Guido, the woman turned man or the woman in process of becoming a man. How broad-minded of Jeremy, Lord Chilcott, the former Conservative politician and pillar of Yorkshire society, to welcome Guido under his roof, he told himself. The British aristocracy had always been good at adapting itself to new social trends. That's why there still was a British aristocracy.

These thoughts occupied Howard until he scrunched his car to a halt on the gravel in front of the mansion. A handsome flight of steps led to the main door on the raised ground floor. Ben answered the bell. He led the way to what Howard remembered as the smoking room. No smoke or smell of tobacco now. Another social trend that the Chilcotts had adapted to, perhaps.

Guido rose to greet him, smiling. He was many years younger than Ben – around thirty – and very Italian. He had been a decent height for a woman and was now a shortish man. Howard was determined not to react to Guido as a freak. Even so, he was astonished at how like a woman Guido looked. The hair was severely cut in the 'short back and sides' style, the chest was flat and the pitch of the voice was contralto. And one would never be able to conceal the shape of the hips and thighs. It added up to a seriously butch woman, but a woman nevertheless. Perhaps the treatment wasn't far advanced.

Ben broke the ice by saying nonchalantly: 'Guido arrived last week. He'll complete the gender reassignment over here.'

This directness – probably a tactic to get the issue out in the open quickly and dealt with – took Howard completely by surprise. His only thought in reply was 'When will the process be completed?' He knew he mustn't go there. *Process* made it sound like a factory production line. All he managed was: 'That's good.'

But was it good for the job to be done over here? He had no idea. Guido clearly thought so. 'I had an assessment yesterday,' he said. His English was almost perfect. 'Everyone was so kind.'

Again Howard was stumped for a response. 'That's nice' seemed inadequate. The question 'When will be the happy day that the treatment is over?' leapt to mind fully formed. It wouldn't do. It might come across as sarcastic or critical. He could think of nothing that wouldn't potentially put him in a quagmire.

Ben came to the rescue. 'How do you like Guido's English?' he said. 'I taught him myself.' Guido smiled as Howard expressed his approval. Ben poured wine – 'good Italian wine, naturally!' – and then joined Guido on the sofa, holding hands. Howard tried not to be distracted. For the moment, Guido looked enough of a woman for hand-holding to pass anywhere in public. The time would come, however, when it would have to stop. Even the big cities in England weren't that evolved. He might have to warn them.

' ... Found a house we think will be suitable.' Guido's words broke in on Howard's private train of thought.

Ben took up the conversation when Howard asked for the point to be repeated. 'We've found a house that we're thinking of buying. It's in Harrogate. Would you see it with us, Howard? We don't know too much about what to look for in England.'

'Good central heating!' said Howard, laughing.

'It's true,' said Guido. 'I've haven't been warm since I came to England. I feel cold in Lowmere even though the heating is on.'

'The aristocracy have to be tough to survive in huge mansions,' Howard joked.

'Then I'm going to have to teach Ben how to survive in a nice, overheated small house,' said Guido.

'I'm only half-aristocratic. My father was a working class boy,' Ben insisted.

'Working class?' Guido was puzzled.

'*Classe operaia,*' said Ben.

All three of them were laughing.

The house was by no means small except by Lowmere standards. It was a handsome Victorian villa with five bedrooms, detached, clearly in good condition and in the heart of the town.

'Do you think people here will accept us as a couple with Guido's background?' Ben asked.

'I'm sure they will,' said Howard. 'British people mostly don't make those sort of judgements any more, least of all in a broad-minded town like this.'

The house was obviously expensive. Ben divulged that, with Guido chipping in a small amount, they had bought the house with money Meg left him. In fact, she left him all her money. Howard had never known the contents of Meg's will, but it gave him an opportunity to launch stage one of his campaign to reconcile her son with his mother's memory. When Guido had wandered off into another room, Howard said to Ben: 'I have something to tell you about your mother. Not now obviously, but can we find a time?'

It was as if steel shutters had rolled down and clanged shut. 'I'm sorry, I can't discuss it,' Ben said. 'Not even with you, Howard.' Usually equable, his expression was thundery, his voice stiff with tension.

'Look, Ben, perhaps I'm presuming but I'm an old man, and the old speak their mind. I loved your mother. Maybe I still love her. I was there – or thereabouts – when you were born. All of that lets me claim the privilege of speaking to you about Meg.'

He saw Ben hesitate. Guido, drawn by the raised voices, returned to the room. 'What's the noise about?' he asked.

'Oh nothing,' said Howard. 'Just a friendly disagreement about the wallpaper in this room.'

'It's dreadful,' Guido pronounced, 'but we'll be repainting all the rooms.'

As they left the house Ben found a space to whisper to Howard that he would meet him, and would he phone to tell him where and when. Howard invited Ben for lunch in the city's main hotel. This was the one where his fiftieth anniversary celebration had been held. He reasoned that the old-fashioned dining room offered plenty of space between the tables. If the conversation turned intimate, as he hoped it would, they wouldn't be overheard.

They talked of everything else except the matter in hand until they were eating their cheese and biscuits. Ben confessed he found it strange to be eating cheese at the end of the meal rather at the start in the Italian way. They laughed, and Howard took advantage of the lighter mood to glide into the subject of Meg. 'This very room, Ben, is where I first talked to your mother. She was a VIP guest at a literary luncheon – a sort of meet-the-author occasion – and I was a junior reporter covering the event. I was immediately smitten.'

'"Smitten"?'

'Swept off my feet,' said Howard, illustrating the words with a sweep of his hands. Ben smiled. 'I know she was very beautiful.'

'She was beautiful but she was also good. She was a good person. She cared about the victims of war and all those who had nothing.' Howard saw he was overdoing it. The steel shutters were rolling down.

'Why do we have to do this?' Ben asked. 'Zia Julia has always been more of a mother to me.'

'I know. I respect that, and I'm not trying to change your feelings for Julia. I want to tell you what happened to me lately. For more than forty years I felt terribly guilty about what I did to your mother. (Shall I just call her "Meg"?) Do you know that we planned to marry, and what happened then?'

'Yes,' said Ben.

'I ran away from the wedding even when Meg was in her wedding gown and all the guests were in the church. I loved her, but I wasn't good enough for her in any way.'

'She wasn't good enough for you, Howard. You're a distinguished man. She would have been lucky to have you.'

'Thank you, Ben, I don't know if that's true now and it certainly wasn't true then. I was dreadfully immature and Meg was already an international film star. I always told myself that by jilting her and turning her life upside down I was to blame for the tragedies of Meg's later years and her ... you know.' He couldn't bring himself to say 'death', much less 'suicide'. 'At times the guilt was unbearable.'

In the way of restaurant staff everywhere, a waiter came to offer coffee at this worst possible moment. Howard waved him away with a 'Later please'.

'Guido says one should see a priest in a situation like that,' Ben interjected.

'I wanted another sort of absolution – from someone who was there and would tell me the truth. I managed to find the one person who could help me – Lucy Plessey.'

'Lucy Plessey!' Ben exclaimed. 'I remember her. She must be very, very old.'

'She is very, very old, but her memory is as sharp as a knife. She showed me that Meg's tragedies were nothing to do with me. They were to do with Everard Hughes and Bob Curzon and how she was treated by the FBI and other things. Lucy said I was irrelevant. The relief was unspeakable!'

Ben smiled. 'To my mother, I was irrelevant too,' he said.

'Oh, but you weren't, Ben. I know she loved you. It must make you unhappy to have bitter feelings towards Meg. Presumptuous of me, I know, but can you not bring yourself to forgive her? The burden will fall away, I promise you.'

'How can you say she loved me when I hardly ever saw her?' Ben asked with bitterness. 'She abandoned me at Lowmere while she went off to her exciting life in London. My first memories are of Julia, not Meg. That's not how it's supposed to be.'

Now Ben's feelings about his mother poured out of him. If the waiters and fellow lunchers wondered at the intensity of the conversation, none gave any sign. Ben spoke about his feelings of abandonment, how he sensed as a young child that his mother preferred to be somewhere other than with him, how he had no memories worth the name of family outings or even of his mother hugging him. As a boy at Eton, he had found her visits strained and a struggle for them both. He had liked Bob Curzon, yet just as they were getting to know each other Bob disappeared from their lives. His feelings as he struggled through the teenage years he shared with Julia. Throughout this long talk at the lunch table, Ben always referred to 'my mother', never 'Mother' or 'Meg'.

Howard sat back and let him talk. 'I know it's been difficult for you, Ben,' he said eventually. 'Meg wasn't perfect. Which of us is? It's taken me years to realise that, despite the surface glamour, she had many difficulties in her life, but I'm sure she never stopped loving you. She was effectively a single mother in London. She left you at Lowmere among all the other people who loved you because she honestly thought it was a better place for you.'

'I'm not sure, Howard. The arrangement was very convenient for her, wasn't it?' 'Ben, I'm sure that was never her motivation.'

Soon after their lunch Ben left for Italy. He explained that Zia Julia was in her final illness, and he would stay with her to the end. Guido went with him. Ben agreed that while he was in Italy he would re-examine his feelings towards his mother. That, Howard told himself, was progress.

# ELEVEN

THE *Messenger* had a board of directors of which Howard was chairman. An international media conglomerate had taken over the newspaper several years ago, leaving the board with little power. Meetings, which were usually boring, comprised a series of departmental reports on matters like circulation figures, advertising campaigns and editorial plans. It was towards the end of one such meeting, and near lunch time. Howard was keen to complete the agenda because Thursday was curry day at the club. Cynthia refused to cook curries. 'Too complicated and besides the turmeric stains everything it touches,' she said.

'Any other business,' Howard announced. 'Nothing then?' He shuffled his papers together and rose from his chair. Most of the others began to follow.

'Excuse me, Chairman. I have an item.' This was Collins, a solicitor and the external director. He was the youngest person on the board. It was most unusual to have anything in AOB. Howard wasn't the only person interested in lunch. 'I want to raise the question of social media,' said Collins.

'What about it?' Howard asked, ungrammatically.

'I've been looking at our Facebook page and following some of the reporters on Twitter,' Collins explained. 'I'm sorry to say the output is pretty unimpressive, particularly compared with our competitors.'

'Tony, this is a big subject at ten to one,' said Howard. He could almost smell the curry. 'Can't we put it on the agenda for next month?'

'With respect, Chairman, I believe there's a degree of urgency about this. We could at least make a start with improving things.'

Howard looked at the four other people in the room. All were men except Anne Crowther (human resources and community outreach). They looked keenly interested, probably less because of the subject than with the prospect of a battle in the making. It would make a welcome change from the usual pedestrian agenda. He accepted the inevitable. He must hope there would be some curry left when he reached the club. He'd known the stuff to run out.

Collins declared that the Facebook page was bland and under-illustrated. Content was slow to be posted. 'For example, that troupe of circus performers went round our office two days ago. The picture still isn't on Facebook.'

Anne Crowther looked angry at this. Facebook was her responsibility although she didn't run the page. But she said nothing.

Collins continued: 'Our readers are encouraged to follow the reporters on Twitter, but some don't seem to be tweeting at all and others are sending messages of the 'what I had for breakfast' kind rather than adding anything to the stories they covered.'

'I suppose they're too busy with stories,' said Howard. 'Surely we need to remember that a reporter's prime responsibility is to write for the paper. We don't want them spending so much time tweeting that their stories suffer.'

'Then why do we invite readers to follow the writers on Twitter?' Collins again.

Rob Willis, the editor, whose area this was, stayed silent.

Howard, ignoring Collins' question that wasn't really a question, went on: 'In any case, a reporter's job is not to peddle their own views. Giving their opinions too freely on Twitter compromises the impartiality of their reports.'

'I don't see why,' retorted Collins. 'News stories are news stories and Twitter is Twitter. Everyone knows the difference.'

'These days readers like to know about the people who write the stories,' Anne Crowther put in.

'We have to move with the times,' observed Jim Murray, the circulation director.

'I don't see that the times are that different. Journalism is still journalism,' said Howard.

This annoyed Collins. 'Chairman, how well do you know our Twitter content?' he asked. 'I suppose you have a Twitter account.'

Howard decided that since it wasn't a question he could ignore it.

'Well?' Collins pursued.

'I know about Twitter.'

'Know *about*. So you don't have a Twitter account?'

Howard agreed he hadn't. 'What about Facebook?' That neither.

Rob Willis cut in: 'Isn't this getting personal? Whether the Chairman has Twitter and Facebook accounts has nothing to do with how our *Messenger* accounts are operated.'

'I wasn't being personal. I was merely trying to clarify the situation,' said Collins disingenuously. 'Chairman, I'd like to propose a motion, that we remind reporters of the importance of frequent tweeting, and ask the Facebook editor to ensure that content is posted in a timely manner.'

'I say,' said Howard, 'isn't that a bit fierce? They'll take it as a direct criticism. Most demoralising. We ought to discuss this matter when we're less rushed. I suggest we pick it up again next month.'

'Nevertheless ...' said Collins.

Howard was obliged to ask whether there was a seconder. Jim Murray raised his hand.

'I want to propose an amendment to take Twitter separately from Facebook,' said Anne Crowther. 'I agree we could do more with Twitter, but the Facebook page is fine.' Howard had a vision of the last of the curry disappearing. The amendment didn't find a seconder.

'Very well, I'll put the original motion to the vote,' he said.

'Can one procedurally have a motion in Any Other Business?' the advertising director, Mike Heaton, piped up. By now Howard was reconciled to the idea of bread and cheese for lunch, but he just wanted to get out of this meeting.

'Oh yes, certainly,' he declared from the chair.

The vote produced a tie. Collins, Murray and Heaton voted for; Jenkins, Willis and Crowther against.

'I give my casting vote against the motion,' said Howard. 'And personally I think that we have the balance right. To do more on Twitter and Facebook would risk damaging our journalism in the newspaper.'

As they all left the room Howard thought he heard Collins mutter *sotto voce* to Murray: 'Not that he'd know anything about it.' But then Howard's hearing was not what it used to be.

He'd won the nasty, brutish duel with Collins. How

was it then, as he said to Cynthia that evening, he felt as if he'd lost? He'd been made to look an old fogey, out of touch with today's touchy-feely journalism, social media and the rest. Perhaps he was an old fogey, out of touch ...

Soon after this meeting news came through that Roger Hudson's Grawton estate had been sold. Sir Roger broke the news himself in a phone call to Howard. The baronet had found his Russian kleptocrat. The buyer was taking on the estate in its entirety – all two and a half thousand acres, with seven tenanted farms, twenty cottages and a public house. 'They'll have to stock more than one brand of vodka now' was Rob Willis' comment.

Sir Roger's cousin Nigel had failed in his High Court bid to prove that the estate was his on an alleged (but unwritten) promise by the previous squire. He retreated to the Virgin Islands, vowing to spill all sorts of family secrets.

'The sale was agreed this afternoon,' Howard told the editor. 'Roger said he liked our previous story, which is why he's giving us this exclusively. He's promised not to tell anyone else until we've published.'

'Excellent!' exclaimed the editor. 'I'll get Emily on to it straight away. We could do a "last sad squire" feature to run alongside the news.'

'Sir Roger is the last squire, but I don't think he's sad,' said Howard. 'He's retiring to Madeira, where he'll have the time of his life.'

'Don't fancy it myself,' said the editor. 'I'd miss the fog and ice and being snowbound.'

'Rob, perhaps I can help. I've known Roger since we were young men. My desk is fairly clear at the moment, so I can do the feature for you if you like.'

Willis thanked him warmly and said he'd get back to him. Howard sat in his office waiting for the call that never came. He waited until seven o'clock, having alerted Cynthia to cancel dinner. 'Big flap on about the Grawton estate,' he told her. He wanted her to know he was still in the thick of things.

A tentative knock on the door was followed by the young reporter who had written the fiftieth anniversary article. He informed Howard that he, the reporter, had been assigned to do a quick feature about the Grawton sale and, because he understood that Sir Howard had known Sir Roger for years, would he, Sir Howard, kindly sketch in some background.

Swallowing his disappointment and his anger, he gave the lad the information he needed. It was another humiliation for Howard – a reminder that the *Messenger* could do very well without him.

A problem remained with Roger. He had told Howard the big news and he expected Howard to write the story. He wasted no time in making that clear when Howard phoned him later that evening. 'I've had a visit by a girl called Emily,' said Roger. 'Charming young person. If I were twenty years younger – but ... But I wanted you. Why did you send her?'

'It was the editor who sent her, Sir Roger. I know she'll do a good job.'

'Not the point. You could have come yourself. You're the boss, aren't you?'

'I suppose I am in a way,' said Howard, 'but the chairman doesn't tell the editor what to do. It's not how it works. I'll tell you what: why don't I come to Grawton tomorrow for a follow-up interview? Should make a good in-depth piece for later.'

He was almost certainly promising more than he could deliver, but he had his own reasons for wanting to see Roger again. By the time Roger realised there wouldn't be a follow-up feature, at least not one written by Howard, he would with luck be so enmeshed with his sale and move that he wouldn't notice. Thus Howard found himself motoring to Grawton for the last time. The Russian kleptocrat might throw lavish parties and receptions; he wouldn't be going to them.

Once again Howard was received by Mrs Matthews, the Grawton housekeeper, with the same impassivity as before. If she recognised him she didn't show it. Once again they traversed the great hall to reach the small sitting room. Sir Roger stood with his back to an unlit hearth, the picture of squirearchical good cheer. 'Welcome. Thank you for coming, Jenkins.' His mood was transformed from their last meeting. Transformed by having offloaded an incubus for many millions, Howard supposed.

'I'm happy to be here, Sir Roger. I hope you liked our coverage this morning of your well deserved sale,' said Howard, gauging (correctly, as it turned out) that he wasn't sticking the *Messenger's* collective chin out for a punch.

'Certainly I did. That Emily's a bright girl. Your competitors liked the articles too. I've had several of them on the phone.'

'We're grateful to you for giving the news to the *Messenger* first. I hope we can build on that now.' Then with his new confidence bestowed by Lucy, Howard added: 'It's a strange world, isn't it, Sir Roger? Many years ago you complained when I wrote a story about you ... yesterday you complained when I didn't write a story about you!'

Roger had also changed. Where once he would have resented the remark, brandished a metaphorical horsewhip, he now smiled. 'It was a long time ago. Things change. People change,' he said.

Emboldened, Howard said: 'I'm sorry Meg came between us.'

Roger gazed at one of his sporting prints on the wall before answering. 'You didn't come between us, Jenkins. Nor for that matter did Haverstock, the wretched Hughes or the rest of Meg's procession of admirers. What came between Meg and me was that I was the boy next door. We knew each other from the year dot. There's no mystery or glamour about the boy next door!'

Howard wondered how many people, if any at all, Roger had shared the thought with. His candour deserved the same in return.

'I suppose no-one came between Meg and me. Not really,' said Howard. 'Everard Hughes was always there, but she knew how undependable he was. Women value dependability, don't they?'

Roger nodded his agreement.

'What came between us,' Howard continued, 'was my awareness of the gulf betweeen us. I could never get over it. She was an aristocrat educated at one of the best schools in England; I was a lower middle class grammar school boy from Bristol. She was famous; I was nobody – a junior reporter.'

'None of that stuff matters,' said Roger.

'It mattered then,' Howard replied. 'In those days, and to me as I was.'

Roger said nothing. They both fell silent, two almost-rivals lost in their respective reveries.

'Sir Howard, have a drink,' said Roger, jerking back to life. 'I suppose when I get to Madeira, being Portuguese, it will have to be port, but while I'm here it's sherry. Will that do you?'

Howard's follow-up article never got written, although other hands at the *Messenger* traced the steady progress of the Grawton sale. Sir Roger departed for Madeira, from where reports filtered back that he was a big hit on the expatriate social circuit. The Russian kleptocrat proved to be a very decent fellow, who filled Grawton with young children (by his third wife). That was the life, Howard reflected, that could have been Meg's and Roger's if she had settled for the boy next door.

# TWELVE

BEN had been in Italy with Guido for several months. Howard heard through the *Messenger's* information network, aka the Hazlitt column, that he was back. He wondered how Ben had got on at Zia Julia's side. He soon found out after he took a call from Lord Chilcott.

Mercifully skipping the empty courtesy of 'How are you?', the peer came straight to the point. 'Howard, I wonder if you'd care to come to Lowmere. Ben's back and he has some news to impart.'

'Jeremy, I'm intrigued.' They had been on first name terms for many years.

'Then come this afternoon. Teatime. It's always teatime at Lowmere!'

Lord Chilcott himself was standing at the open front door when Howard reached the house. He shook hands warmly. 'Thank you so much, Howard,' he said. 'The family will always be in your debt.'

'What on earth have I done?' a mystified Howard asked lightly.

'You'll soon find out from Ben. He's in the Orangery with Guido. Celia and I will join you for tea a little later.' Celia was Lady Chilcott.

The two younger men both rose to greet Howard. Guido looked and sounded exactly as he had before – like a very butch woman. The treatment, if it had continued in Italy, had yet to produce much external effect.

'I'm sorry to say that Zia Julia died,' said Ben. 'It was a long illness but she was peaceful at the end.' 'That's what matters,' Howard mumbled.

'Sadly, she wasn't so very old,' Guido put in tactlessly.

'Yet she had a life full of love,' said Ben. He blinked back tears. Howard wondered what all this had to do with him. Ben explained. 'I asked Zia about my mother. I hadn't done that before. I don't know why. Zia said my mother was a fine person and I should honour her.' He looked at Guido for encouragement.

'I told you that before Zia Julia did,' Guido said, taking his partner's hand. 'Everyone should honour his mother and his father. It's in the Bible.'

'In fact, it was Zia Julia's dying wish that I should love the memory of my mother. I told Zia that it felt disloyal to her. She said I could love both of them. It wasn't a competition.'

'I never thought it was a competition,' said Howard. 'I'm so delighted to hear this, Ben.'

'And I'm changing my name,' Ben added matter of factly.

'Oh, that's a surprise. I've always like "Benjamin" as a name.'

'I mean my last name. From now on I'm "Denby", not "Hughes". I've got more reason to thank my mother than my father, haven't I? It's all thanks to you, Howard,' Ben continued. 'You told me how Lucy had made you see right about Meg. That started me thinking. I had plenty of time to think as I watched poor Zia fade away.' He walked over to Howard and wrapped him in a warm embrace. Howard, who had observed young Britons hugging but hadn't practised the art himself, was even more embarrassed when Guido did the same.

'Howard, you have so many memories of Meg,' Ben said. 'I want you to tell me everything, absolutely everything.'

'Whenever you like and for as long as you like!'

At the top of his voice Ben bellowed: 'Uncle Jeremy, ready now!'

'Whatever happened to the servants' bell?' Howard joked.

'No servants ... well, not many!' Ben replied.

Jeremy and his wife came into the Orangery, with Celia pushing a tea trolley. 'Coffee, tea or me?' she cried. Howard smiled. Ben and Guido looked puzzled. 'It was a book,' she explained. 'A long time ago. About air hostesses.'

Lord Chilcott shook Howard's hand again. 'Ben's explained, I believe. We'll always be grateful. A rift in the family is so painful. Now, let's not talk about it anymore.'

Later, Jeremy asked Howard apparently out of the blue: 'How many films did my sister make?' He was told about twenty. "And there were some good ones?'

'Lots of good ones,' said Howard. 'One in particular, *As Far as the Eye Can See*, was a huge hit in France. It was hailed as a seminal picture of the Sixties ... a sort of *Breathless* for London. The French are never wrong about films!' Everyone laughed.

"Tell Sir Howard about your idea, Ben,' said Lord Chilcott.

'It was Zia Julia's idea, actually,' Ben explained. 'She said it was right to honour Mamma in the place that meant so much to her, and it would also celebrate me returning to live in England. Zia was sad about that, but she knew it was what I wanted after she had passed on.'

'I think it's a splendid idea,' said Celia. 'We'll show a few of Meg's best films, and have talks and seminars. I'm sure people who knew her and worked with her will attend.'

Jeremy added: 'Somebody asked me in York the other day whether Meg Denby was related to our family. Time to put her on the map again!' Ben explained to a puzzled Guido: 'Make her well known again.'

Howard also thought a festival was a splendid idea. He promised that the *Messenger* would sponsor it – 'What better cause ... Yorkshire girl for a Yorkshire newspaper?' – and between them they would become a team to organise it. Ben and Guido would do the administrative legwork, Howard would look after publicity and arrange the films and speakers, Jeremy would get local notabilities on board to give the event 'bottom' and Celia would take the most important job of all – food and drink.

His wife wasn't enthused when Howard excitedly told her about the festival. 'Howie, don't you think you're becoming obsessed with Meg Denby? I suppose Ben coming home has done it.'

'The festival wasn't my idea, Cyn. Honest. It was Ben's – and Aunt Julia's.'

Cynthia ploughed on: 'Then again, I suppose you've always been obsessed with Meg Denby. I'm well used to playing second fiddle.'

'Cyn, you know that's not true.' But they both knew it was.

'Second fiddle to a ghost ... that's harder than with a real woman.' They knew that was true, too.

'Cynthia, it's a beastly thing to say.' He couldn't just forget she'd invoked that image, and nor was she disposed to apologise. The rest of the evening passed in a strained atmosphere. Howard resolved not to mention the festival again.

Preparations got underway immediately. Howard

admired the energy of Ben and Guido, who drew up marketing plans, created website content, devised booking procedures – and at the same time moved house. Their new home exuded an air of manic activity. Upstairs a pair of painters were recolouring walls and builders were installing an en-suite for the master bedroom. Below, more builders were knocking down the wall between the sitting room and the dining room. The two owners were to be found in the only part of the house not so far affected by these refurbishments – a small bedroom that was the festival office. The desk had already acquired a clutter of papers, which partly submerged the all-important laptop. They had acquired from somewhere two posters for Meg's films, and had pinned them on the walls.

'Welcome to the nerve centre of the festival!' said Ben.

'I'm impressed,' Howard replied. 'As I am with all your improvements (waving a hand to suggest the painters and builders).'

We thought it was a good idea to have everything done at once,' said Guido. Ben added: 'But perhaps it wasn't such a good idea. Neither of us can sleep. Our heads are too full of what we want to do next. With the house and with the festival.'

Howard sympathised. 'I know the feeling,' he said – although in truth it was a long time since he'd lain awake churning over creative ideas. As they had coffee, he asked the pair how they liked Harrogate.

'We love it,' said Guido. 'Except the weather,' Ben joked.

Guido explained: 'It's rather small, but it feels like a city. Lots of Italian cities are like that. I feel at home. Everyone is so friendly.'

Ben nodded. 'You're not surprised at that, Howard? We were. Everyone knows our story from the *Sun* article. Little things slip out, but you know what – nobody cares.'

'Just what I told you about modern Britain,' said Howard.

The effects of Guido's treatment became ever more apparent. Howard noticed more hair on the arms, a deepening of the voice, a tautening of the previously feminine physique. Only occasionally was there a gesture or an action that was essentially feminine, as when Guido touched him on the forearm to emphasise a point he was making.

Ben and Guido always seemed to be together. Maybe, thought Howard, they would be one of those rare couples who in fifty years had never spent a night apart. Well, given Ben's age make that thirty years ...

They were together, as always, when they came into the *Messenger* office to see Howard on festival business. Ben waved to Emily as they walked through the reporters' room.

'Who was that fanciable man with Ben?' she asked Howard later. He told her. 'Guido!' she exclaimed. 'I would never have known it.' 'That's the idea,' said Howard lightly. 'Good luck to them,' Emily replied stoutly.

The weekend of the Meg Denby Celebration Film Festival was dry and warm. More than two hundred festivaliers with a respectable showing of journalists from the national press enjoyed the Lowmere grounds, which were looking their best. It was the sort of occasion that few do as well as the English and none do better. The ancient stones of the mansion were bathed in sunshine.

Most of the events were being held in the main drawing room, whose French windows stood wide open. On the lawn beyond the terrace a tea tent had been erected to serve teas, coffees, snacks savoury or sweet and – Celia's triumph – a huge variety of cakes.

At the opening ceremony a tribute from Lucy Plessey was shown. Lucy apologised that old age and infirmity meant she couldn't make the long journey from Devon to Yorkshire. She described Meg as her best friend and hoped she could call herself the same in reverse. She still missed Meg; in fact, she thought about her every day. She believed the films to be shown would demonstrate that Meg was a better actress than she was sometimes given credit for. She, Lucy, hoped that the festival would also remember Meg's work for the underprivileged and the discriminated against – Vietnamese, British miners and women everywhere. This simple and moving video clip earned a huge round of applause.

Benjamin Denby, formerly Hughes, then spoke with Guido at his side. Ben said how proud he was that his mother's films were remembered and that so many were gathered here in the place that she loved best. It was no secret that they had been estranged for many years, but he now knew how wrong he had been. As he proceeded his Italian-accented English became more pronounced. He concluded by looking skywards and declaring: 'Mother – Mamma – please forgive me!' At this, Guido took his hand. The crowd applauded wildly.

The four films selected for screening were considered to represent some of Meg's best: *All in a Day's Work* (in which she burst on the world as a delightful ingénue and during the filming of which she fell for Everard Hughes); *As Far as the Eye Can See* (her most famous picture);

*One Swallow at Midsummer* (from the novel of the same name by Arnold Haverstock), and the late-period *Tug of Love*, which the critics had retrospectively rescued from turkeydom.

The films, each shown twice the better to comprehend them, were interspersed with talks and social gatherings (no extra charge). Earnest academics deconstructed the four pictures and offered assessments of Meg Denby's career overall. Stars who had worked with Meg proved hard to find – in fact, impossible. They were dead, not interested, incorrigibly alcoholic or, in the case of Bob Curzon, tactfully not invited.

At this point, Howard had had a brainwave. 'What about Bert Brump? He was the director of Meg's biggest hit.'

'He was pretty old at the time,' said Jeremy. 'I remember Meg saying so. He must be well dead by now.' But ninety-six-year-old Bert Brump wasn't dead. What's more, the spry nonagenarian would be delighted to speak at the festival, where his self-deprecatory style was to prove one of the hits of the occasion.

Meg's character in *As Far as the Eye Can See* plays an estate agent who sells a small flat to someone she thinks is an ordinary man able to afford nothing more. It turns out that he's a millionaire buying the property for his niece. He is so impressed with Meg's energy and commitment to a small deal that he also buys a country estate with land stretching literally as far as the eye can see – and marries his estate agent.

Dismissed by the London critics as trivial and derivative, the picture was predictably a mega-hit. Under the title *Le secret d'un veuf* (A Widower's Secret), it was hailed in France where critics believed they found hidden depths.

'Mr Brump,' the auteur was asked during his question and answer session, '*As Far as Anyone Knows* has been the subject of critical reappraisal in recent years both in this country and the United States. Why do you think that is?'

'Speak up!' the director replied. 'I only hear the easy questions.' Laughter.

The question was repeated. Bert responded promptly: 'The French. They know about these things.' More laughter. 'I thought I was making a low-budget weepie: boy meets girl – misunderstandings – misunderstandings cleared up – boy marries girl. Turns out I was making ... what does it say?' He turned to Howard, who was chairing the session, and asked him to read from a sheet of paper. ' My eyes, you know,' adding in a whisper: 'The yellow bits.' With Bert Brump it was often unclear when he was being genuine and when he was acting.

Howard read out: 'a disquisition on social fluency and democracy. The spirit of young London isn't confined to the rich and well connected. The miniskirt is available to all'; 'the plot is trite, no doubt deliberately so, but this apparent comedy is really about the English social order'; 'a subtle and well directed attack on the English class system where estates of the size depicted continue to exist, and the only way an ordinary person can share in them is by accident'; 'a trenchant statement about the nature of chance'; 'a richly layered picture with meta-narratives well worth the effort of unpicking. The film's philosophical underpinnings place it in the Berkeleyan mould on the nature of reality.'

'Hope you got all that,' said Bert. 'If I'd known the picture was that important I'd have tried harder.' Laughter.

'Mr Brump, the plot was just described as "deliberately trite". Is it *deliberately* trite?' 'It is now,' the auteur replied. More laughter.

'Mr Brump, how do you evaluate Meg Denby's performance in *As Far as We Can Tell?*'

'I wanted a girl next door type and no one could play the girl next door better than Meg.' With a sweeping gesture he pointed through the open French doors to the park. 'Marvellous really. She didn't know much about next-doors herself. They call it acting.' Laughter.

And so it went on. The paradox was that talking down his film was probably the best way to cement its reputation. Howard wondered whether the auteur did it knowingly or was simply being himself.

After the showing of *Tug of Love*, Howard found himself walking behind an elderly clergyman towards the tea tent. 'What did you make of the picture?' he asked by way of conversation as they joined the queue. In the film Meg plays the mother of a teenage daughter whose rows with her step-father are destroying the marriage. Meg's character faces the agony of having to choose between the two people she loves.

'I found it most moving,' the clergyman replied.

'It was ahead of its time in focusing on the problems of step-families, of which there are so many nowadays,' said Howard. The clergyman agreed that so-called 'blended families' often gave rise to problems. It was, he observed, one of the biggest social issues today.

They agreed to sit together while they enjoyed their tea and cakes. Howard selected a seat a little away from the crowd. To his surprise he saw the man's eyes were moist. He was dabbing them with a handkerchief. 'I shouldn't have come,' he said mostly to himself.

Howard's career as a journalist had left him rarely at a loss for words, even if they weren't always the right ones. Should he mention the man's distress and thereby call attention to it? At last he said: 'It was indeed a most moving film. I'm sure Meg' – to everyone at the festival she was "Meg" – 'would have been delighted.'

'And she would have known the reason.' To this obscure remark Howard found nothing to say. He decided to introduce himself, as strangers invariably do, if they do at all, after many exchanges. 'Howard Jenkins.' 'Bob Curzon.'

'What a coincidence,' said Howard. 'Same name as Meg's co-star.' Something stopped him. He looked at the man again. 'You *are* Bob Curzon!' So Bob was there after all. Unrecognised and unrecognisable. Uninvited, he had nevertheless felt driven to attend.

Bob required little prompting to pour out his story. He had met Meg in that glorious springtime for them all when they made *As Far as the Eye Can See*. In what he supposed was a rarity among stars on location, they didn't have an affair although they enjoyed one night of love on the last day of the shoot. Years later they were reunited for *Tug of Love*. Then they became seriously a couple.

'Everyone remarks how realistic the love scenes are ... that's because they *were* real!' said Bob, interrupting himself.

He had left his wife Meryl long before while Meg had had a succession of short-term partners. They soon began living together. This was where the problems began. He struggled to cope with her moods and increasingly abandoned drinking and drug-taking. He loved her, but he could no longer live with her. To his shame he returned to his wife. Within months Meg was dead. His marriage failed again. He had been alone ever since. He had never made another picture since *Tug of Love*, had never wanted to. The church seemed to offer some chance of making sense of it all. He applied and was accepted for holy orders.

Bob was weeping freely now. Some bystanders noticed. Howard, taking Bob by the elbow, led him to a quieter part of the grounds.

'I've always blamed myself for Meg's death,' Bob sobbed. 'It's with me all the time. I abandoned her when she needed me most.'

'You mustn't blame yourself. I'm sure there were many factors that led her to take her own life,' said Howard.

'I won't have it!' said Bob with heat. 'I and I only am to blame. If I had stayed with her it wouldn't have happened. Do you know that a stranger almost saved her at Flamborough Head? He ran a hundred yards to reach her and pull her away from the edge. He was only five yards away when she ... threw herself over. That for me is the cruellest thought. Five more yards and she would be here today. The idea haunts me.'

Howard said: 'I too found I couldn't forgive myself for something I did to someone else, who then died. I found that person's closest friend. She convinced me that it wasn't my fault at all ... that, unknown to me, I was irrelevant to the situation ...'

'How can you say I was irrelevant?' Bob protested.

'Most certainly I'm not saying that,' Howard replied. 'I'm giving the example because the friend's remarks were an absolution ... yes, a secular absolution.'

'As a priest I know all about absolution,' said Bob. 'In my case, I want absolution from God. I've asked for it and I suppose I have it. The trouble is we never really know, do we? I continue to hope and pray that I may hear His word clearly.'

Howard didn't think it was his place to talk to a priest about faith. Instead, he said: 'I think Meg would absolve you too.'

'That's a very helpful idea. I'm grateful for it,' said Bob. By now he had recovered himself. 'Thanks for listening. Perhaps it's time to go back for the next event. Did you know Meg yourself by any chance?'

'I saw something of her when I was a young reporter here,' said Howard. 'She was a beautiful person in every possible way.'

The festival attracted much attention in the Twittersphere when it was running and for many days afterwards. The tweeters were mainly full of praise for the event and for Meg. 'A brilliant actress – why haven't we seen more of her? and 'cool at lowmeer [misspelt] – another next yr pls' were typical comments. Many people supported Ben for the honesty of his speech, and a few were hostile to Meg. 'You'll feel better ben – everyone needs a mum!' and 'not your fault ben – she desserted [misspelt] you remember' were typical of this strand.

All these remarks passed by Howard, who still didn't do Twitter. Emily, who did, assured him that there was lots of reaction and that it was overwhelmingly favourable.

Thanks to Howard's publicity, the festival was well attended by critics from the upmarket and middle market London media. Even the mass market *Sun* and *Mir-*

*ror* mentioned it as a forthcoming event although they didn't send critics. The *Daily Telegraph's* article was the best of the invariably positive reviews:

## MEG DENBY, THE STAR WE WRONGLY FORGOT

IN the beautiful setting of Lowmere Abbey, her much-loved childhood home, a three-day festival has celebrated the life and work of the late actress Meg Denby.

Denby, who took her own life in 1985, left us with around 20 films, of which four were shown at the festival. They included her international mega-hit, *As Far as the Eye Can See,* and, arguably her best, the late-period *Tug of Love.*

While on the face of it most of her pictures were mere frothy entertainments (but not *Tug of Love*) the scorchingly beautiful Denby played her parts to perfection – and brought out strands of social realism that we as critics have been slow to see. The French got there first when on first release they hailed *As Far as the Eye Can See* as a tale of 'human relations through the prism of class and the role of fate', and the like.

The mini-skirted spirit of Swinging London comes to life in this story of an estate agent who wins the heart of a millionaire in disguise by treating him as just another buyer. In this and her other films, Meg Denby emerges as the true voice of the Sixties.

The matter was expressed to perfection by Denby's director on the picture, 96-year-old Bert Brump. He told the festival: 'I wanted a girl next door type and no one could play the girl next door better than Meg.'

As Denby showed us, however, girls-next-door are not mere airheaded cuties. They have hearts and brains, too. A decade and a half on and we find a darker Denby in *Tug of Love*. Here she plays a mother in a household from hell torn between her teenage daughter and her second husband. Artfully, Denby overlays her familiar ingénue persona with the anguish of a mature woman plumbing the depths of life.

Clearly, we as critics and cinema-going public have greatly underrated Denby as an artist. Last weekend's festival was a major step to putting this right.

It is worth noting that Denby's Hollywood career foundered when the FBI objected to her political campaigning. She was a vocal opponent of the Vietnam War, later supporting women's lib (an early form of feminism) and, at the time of her death, the striking miners. Denby's projected part in *A Multicolored Rose* was handed to Alison Adams, the enduring Tinseltown A-lister – and a lesser actress.

The organising committee of Howard, Jeremy, Celia, Ben and Guido met at Lowmere a few days after the festival. They had before them the large pile of press cuttings collected by Howard's secretary. After they had pored over the material with pleasure bordering in some cases on incredulity, Jeremy expressed the feeling of them all. He said: 'This festival achieved what I scarcely dared hope for – justice for Meg.'

# THIRTEEN

HOWARD had a visitation from Cartwright, the Corporate HQ principal bean counter, as he thought of him. He had never liked Cartwright and he could safely suppose that the head office man didn't like him. In his more charitable moments Howard told himself that neither of them was at fault. As a chartered accountant and chief financial officer, Cartwright was almost bound to dislike journalists with their free-wheeling, free-spending approach to life.

As Cartwright had been heard to say more than once: 'Other departments make money, editorial spends it.' He was a small, bespectacled man in late middle age – a stereotype, in fact, of a certain type of chartered accountant. He was also the son of a press photographer who had deserted the family home, an experience that may have envenomed the boy's views of journalism.

Today as usual, Cartwright walked through the office with a faintly disapproving air of a man always on guard against someone trying to put something over on him. He settled himself into a chair in Howard's office without being invited to sit. Howard didn't like this. It was as if Cartwright thought of the place as his. In a sense it was, but proprieties must be maintained.

After Marcia, the chairman's secretary, had brought coffee, Cartwright opened with a general observation: 'This is a difficult time for newspapers, Sir Howard.' For years it had been 'Mr Cartwright' and 'Mr Jenkins' (and then 'Sir Howard'). Howard agreed it was, with so much emphasis on digital and so much advertising migrating to the internet.

'Of course, the digital spend is available to us as it is to everyone else,' Cartwright mused. 'How do you feel our digital proposition is doing?'

Howard replied: 'Like everyone else we're struggling to find a model that replaces digitally the revenues we lose from falling print sales. But I believe we're doing pretty well as a, so to speak, work in progress.'

'I'm afraid that's not what our comparables tell us, Sir Howard,' said Cartwright. '*Messenger* print circulation and therefore revenues are down disproportionately to our other titles. Digital income is growing less than we would expect for the size of the operation. Social media seem to be a particular problem area.'

He paused. Howard said nothing. Cartwright continued: 'Sir Howard, you lead the board, which will take its line from you. What's your policy on social media?'

'We're highly committed to it as a way of promoting the *Messenger*.'

'In theory or in practice?' 'In both, Mr Cartwright.' Howard wondered whether Tony Collins, the board member who had tussled with him over Facebook, had somehow got to Cartwright. The next question more or less proved it. 'But you yourself perhaps aren't an active user, with a Facebook page and the rest of it?'

'I believe my time is better spent on oversight and advice rather than directly using social media myself.' He could see Cartwright wasn't impressed with this answer. They talked on. Howard was aware that he was being held to account. Certainly the financial numbers were dire: spelt out by Cartwright, they were worse than he had realised.

'Then you've just held the Meg Denby film festival.'

Here Cartwright paused for dramatic effect. 'Which the *Messenger* supported to the tune of fifty thousand pounds.'

His implication was clear. 'Worth every penny for the newspaper in publicity and goodwill,' said Howard. 'Meg Denby was a famously beautiful Yorkshire film star – and from one of our leading county families. Her brother is Lord Chilcott.'

'Hmm. The payment was made without board approval, I believe,' Cartwright pursued.

Howard replied: 'I notified the board, but I don't believe it needed their approval. As executive chairman I discussed it with the chief accountant. She drew the sum from the authorised promotional budget.'

'Be that as it may, would it perhaps have been wise to run it past the board – range of views, you know – given that it's an enormous sum to spend without any measurable financial return? Sir Howard, I believe you have personal connections with the Chilcott family,' here Cartwright delivered another dramatic pause, 'and with Meg Denby.'

One of Howard's enemies on the board must have fed that to head office.

'Mr Cartwright, I must ask you to withdraw the imputation that I used this money improperly because of my friendship with Lord Chilcott and his family.'

'Sir Howard, I never meant to suggest that, but to the extent that you misunderstood my comment I withdraw it.' They both knew that Howard hadn't misunderstood.

They had been talking for the better part of an hour when Cartwright gave signs of leaving. 'Thank you for the update, Sir Howard – and thank you as always for your commitment to this newspaper.' He cleared his throat. Howard wondered what was coming. 'You've given many years of distinguished service. Don't you think now would be a good time to enjoy the fruits of all that hard work? Travel, golf, gardening ... so many things that work gets in the way of, eh?'

'I'll certainly think about it.'

'Perhaps you should do more than think about it, Sir Howard.' A hard look made his meaning clear if it had been in doubt. 'Now if you'll excuse me ...' He picked up his coat and briefcase, and was gone. Howard left the office soon after Cartwright. He drove home on autopilot, reeling with the memory of what he'd been told.

Cynthia was amazed to find him home at that time of day. 'Cyn, I've been sacked.'

'Sacked? What do you mean "sacked"?'

'Sacked. Fired. Pushed out. What is there not to understand about "sacked"?'

He stifled a sob. She drew him to her in an uncharacteristically warm embrace. 'Howie, I'm so sorry' is all she said. He told her how Corporate HQ had complained about his financial management and his spending on the film festival. He reminded her of the mess he'd made of stories about Benjamin Hughes and Roger Hudson's estate.

'What a hash I've made of things!' he exclaimed. 'I'm finished. To think that after all these years it's come to this.'

The phone rang. It was 10 Downing Street. A well modulated voice said: 'Sir Howard, for your distinguished service to the newspaper industry and the journalism profession, the Prime Minister would like to offer you a peerage.'

## THE END

# ACKNOWLEDGEMENTS

Many thanks to Paul Hopkins, Margaret Hopkins, Michael Coates-Smith and Gerald Knight for their careful reading of the manuscript of this novel, and their helpful suggestions. Any mistakes of fact or judgement are entirely the author's. Many thanks also to Jude Brent-Khan for proof-reading the text.

The facts of the miners' strike of 1984-85 have been imaginatively reconstructed, and are seen in this story from Meg's perspective. Information is drawn from many sources, with special acknowledgement to Wikipedia. Ituri Publications actively supports the not-for-profit Wikimedia Foundation, which owns the free online encyclopaedia. Wikipedia welcomes donations, small or large: **www.wikipedia.org/**

**If you liked *Coda for a Star* please tell your friends about it! Ituri is an independent publishing house without the marketing budget of the giant corporations. (If you didn't like this novella please tell us – ituribooks@yahoo.co.uk/ All messages will be answered.)**

## *When the impossible happens ...*

If you enjoyed this book, read a prequel (the first in the Meg Denby trilogy)

# Girl at the Top Table
## By Martin Horrocks

Journalist Howard Jenkins glimpses the gorgeous film star Meg Denby at a literary event, and is hit almost senseless. During the 1967 'Summer of Love', he embarks on a fevered chase in Yorkshire and London to get to know her — but how is an ordinary bloke to succeed with a girl like that?

Available from Ituri (**www.ituri.co.uk**) for £4.99, post-free within the UK, or from bookshops. (Ask us for the postage cost on foreign orders.) ISBN 9780957147980. *Girl at the Top Table* is also available as an ebook from Amazon